Line Fall River

The Old Colony

Pilgrim land - past and present

Line Fall River

The Old Colony
Pilgrim land - past and present

ISBN/EAN: 9783337294885

Printed in Europe, USA, Canada, Australia, Japan

Cover: Foto ©Andreas Hilbeck / pixelio.de

More available books at **www.hansebooks.com**

THE OLD COLONY;

OR,

PILGRIM LAND,

PAST AND PRESENT.

The Arrival of the Mayflower

ISSUED BY THE

FALL RIVER LINE AND OLD COLONY RAILROAD.

1887.

CONTENTS.

	PAGES.
PILGRIM LAND,	3
FALL RIVER LINE,	6
NEWPORT,	14
NANTASKET AND ITS NEIGHBORHOOD,	22
SOUTH SHORE,	29
PLYMOUTH,	34
MASSACHUSETTS BAY,	39
CAPE COD,	50
MARTHA'S VINEYARD,	58
NANTUCKET,	63
BUZZARD'S BAY, — ONSET, AND ALONG SHORE,	71
HERE AND THERE,	75
HOTELS AND BOARDING-HOUSES,	85
HOW TO GET THERE,	96

MAPS.

GENERAL MAP OLD COLONY RAILROAD,	opp.	Title.
NEWPORT,	"	16
CAPE COD, — LOWER END,	"	50
MARTHA'S VINEYARD AND SECTION OF CAPE COD,	"	58
NANTUCKET,	"	68

THE PILGRIM LAND.

N the early days of American history, all the population of what afterwards became the United States lived near the Atlantic coasts; and for many years after the formation of the confederacy of commonwealths the inhabitants had penetrated but comparatively a short distance inland, so that the ocean, with its indenting bays and sounds, and the rivers emptying into it along every part of the coast, furnished always attractive facilities for transportation and habitation purposes, while water-fronts were easy of access in summer, even for that portion of the population most remote from the shores, and the delights of the element were available for a people seemingly almost amphibious by nature, by history and practice, belonging nearly as much to the water as to the land, and which had little idea of recreative or diverting exercises that were not conducted near the seashore.

Although the people of the United States are at present scattered far and wide over countless square miles of country, until they have occupied nearly every portion of a territory lying between two great oceans 3,000 miles apart from east to west, and with an expanse from north to south nearly as great, they have never yet lost, have scarcely modified, in fact, the distinguishing traits of their early history, at least with reference to their love of ocean and water scenery and situations. "Watering-places," localities by lake or river or sea-shore, are as much a necessity north, east, south and west, in this country, as are township organizations or cemeteries. Nor have the descendants of the fathers rooted out or discouraged the ancient love for ocean haunts and seashore resorts which first prevailed; and to this day pilgrimages to the ocean front are made from every inland section during the warm months, the devotees travelling thousands of miles, and numbering hundreds of thousands of souls yearly, in gratification of this inherent desire.

And so, in process of time, favorable or attractive situations upon the Atlantic coasts have become well known, even famous, among communities a thousand or two thousand miles away from the sound of surf-beat or sight of rolling billow; and it has come to pass that people of these inland sections know the seashores better than some who dwell within reach of ocean breezes. Thus for upwards of thirty years in succession a goodly company of Clevelanders have sought out with the return of every summer an enchanting seashore retreat among the hills and dunes of old Plymouth; St. Louis pilgrims have baited the bluefish or steered the yacht in the blue Nantucket waters; and thousands of denizens of the far West have animated almost every mile of our coast line.

Among the sections of shore line thus distinguished and favored from Maine to Texas, none present more of intrinsic merit, viewed from any standpoint, than those of south-eastern Massachusetts. Having nearly the oldest, and by far the most striking, history in the country, their associations in this direction are far beyond that which attaches elsewhere, and these claims never fail to receive the consideration of all intelligent persons. The Rock of Plymouth; the lands trodden by the feet of the Pilgrim Fathers; the homes of Samoset and Massasoit, and the Indian tribes which made famous every foot of shore from Mount Wollaston away round to Penekeese and the Island of Rhode; the birth-place of the great fishing and whaling interests; the districts of the stern Puritan and Quaker religions; the burial-place of Presidents; the homes and haunts of the Adamses, Webster, and a host of other men famous in the annals of great achievements—all these present superior inducements. And, besides, in the natural endowments and attractions of the section : the glorious beauties of its frowning bluffs; its wooded hills coming down often to the very water's edge; its white-gleaming beaches; its rock-bound shores; its bays and coves, harbors and roadsteads; its unrivalled ocean views and outlooks; its facilities for fishing and fowling, and sporting and pleasuring; its dotting islands, often isolated bits of seemingly ideal creation; and the miles upon miles succeeding of charming scenery and situations stretching inland from the shores. Cool forest driveways; innumerable lakes and ponds for fishing or fowling; streams for "trouting;" historic hills for climbing, and plains for exploration—and above and beyond all, a summer climate of unequalled sanitary advantages; air bracing and invigorating like magic tonics; bubbling springs of purest water at every turn; miles upon miles of the finest beaches anywhere to be found in existence for salt or fresh water bathing; all these and many more advantages distinguish this section, long since brought it into favorable notice, and are now rapidly revolutionizing the whole expanse, turning it bit by bit into the summer haunts of pilgrims from every State and region.

Measured by the twistings and windings of the shores, South-eastern Massachusetts has upwards of 300 miles of continuous seacoast between the points named above, possessing in almost every part the characteristics before enumerated. If there were nothing to attract thitherward during the summer season any objects more magnetic than the two beautiful islands of Nantucket and Martha's Vineyard, lying respectively forty and fifteen miles off the coast, the tide of visitation would still set strongly in this direction: but these are only supplementary to the seductive invitations of the main-land.

Formerly the white-winged "packet," plying busily from port to port and from point to point, furnished both means of communication and transportation for humanity and merchandise along these shores. Lumbering stage-coaches (not yet entirely abolished in some obscure districts, and often running amid scenes of surpassing loveliness, as in many Cape Cod localities) rattled over the woods' roads, or toiled laboriously along their sandy highways. At present there is scarcely a furlong of these hundreds of miles of seacoast that is not directly included in the ministrations of the Old Colony Railroad, which has "gridironed" this south-eastern section in every part. Foreseeing what has actually happened, that the summer pilgrims of every State, and especially those more or less inland, would inevitably discover what treasures this section held in store, and what prodigality of delights had been lavished by natural provision here, the management of this transportation system has carried its lines into every part, leaving out no appreciable attraction, neglecting no favored or commendable locality. Its sumptuous trains, with the regularity of the sunbeams and the sea breezes, dart about among these varying and ever beautiful scenes, connecting with steamboats which duplicate in every way upon the water the functions of the railroad upon the land, or with coaches and auxilliaries which, first and last, satisfy the wants and demands of every class of travellers.

THE FALL RIVER LINE.

HE "Fall River Line" is the descriptive title of a transportation enterprise whose prime factors are the Old Colony Steamboat Company, occupying Long Island Sound and Mount Hope Bay, and the Old Colony Railroad system, which traverses every part of the territory of South-eastern Massachusetts, and whose lines extend very nearly to the New Hampshire boundaries, through the eastern sections of the Old Bay State. Although these companies are distinct in their organization, the same management (the same persons) appears in both, and they are identical in all purposes, features of direction and general characteristics. The great boats of the Old Colony Steamboat Company — the Pilgrim, Bristol, Providence, etc., — traverse the entire length of Long Island Sound and Mount Hope Bay, connecting New York with Newport and Fall River; and from the last-named cities the train-service of the Old Colony Railroad continues this traffic directly with Boston and all eastern points, the union of service, as has already been stated above, constituting the "Fall River Line" between New York and Boston.

Now the name of this Line, and generally the quality and importance of its services as a transportation agency, have become familiar in every part of the country; and the fame of its wonderful steamboats has gone out through all the earth, foreign journals often taking occasion to refer to or describe them as among the notable institutions of the time. Since its establishment literally millions of patrons have been carried safely and comfortably by its combined land and water service, and its record is written in the experiences of travellers representing every state and country of the earth, the number of whom is Legion. Its peculiar advantages, the luxury of its appointments, the safety of all its appliances, its wonderful record with regard to freedom from accidents and casualties, its great floating hotels, affording all the accommodations of a first-class caravansary to travellers, the fascination and attractions of its routes — all these and many other characteristics long since commended it to the public, and it is now many decades since the Fall River Line took place as the foremost transportation enterprise of its kind upon the globe. That this statement is true all experienced travellers will attest; and the novice may at any time establish the fact for himself.

The passenger fleet of steamboats belonging to the Fall River Line (the freight boats form a department by themselves) is comprised of the steamers "Pilgrim," "Bristol," "Providence," "Old Colony" and "Newport," and during the time that summer flitting is "on," all these

THE "PILGRIM" IN THE EAST RIVER.

vessels are in commission, and are taxed to their utmost capacity in serving the travel between New York, Newport, Boston and the East, and correspondingly between Boston, the North and East, and New York and the West. The "Pilgrim," from the moment she took place in the Line, has been known as the "Iron Monarch of Long Island Sound," and no one has ever in the least doubted her right to assume, or her ability to justify, this title. Built by the world-renowned firm of John Roach & Sons, the length of this enormous craft is 390 feet; width over guards, 88 feet; depth, 18 feet 6 inches; measurement from top of dome to base line, 60 feet. Her normal speed is 20 miles per hour. Her cost was upwards of $1,000,000. In build she is a ship within a ship, having two iron hulls, so constructed that she has all the real strength of a vessel equalling in thickness of hull the measurement from her inner to the outer shell. Between the two hulls there are 96 water-tight compartments, and within the ship seven water-tight compartments; and it is simply impossible to sink this steamer through any known form of accident.

The Pilgrim has sleeping accommodations for 1,200 passengers. She is lighted with 1,000 incandescent electric lights, aggregating 12,000 candles, and Mr. Edison has exhausted his inventive faculties in fitting up this magnificent vessel. In her construction all known modern improvements have been supplied and utilized, and from any nautical stand-point she is perfect and complete in every department.

Of the interior arrangements, decorations, appliances, fittings and furnishings of the "Pilgrim," it can only be said that they are indeed palatial, with all that can be implied by that term. Her grand saloons, cabins, state-rooms, social halls, dining-saloons, offices, every provision in fact, are equal to anything found in the fitting of the most elegant caravansary on land, while many of her appointments are unique and peculiar to the duties she performs as an ocean carrier. Every department of her service is of the same exalted character, and one may order freely, with the same certainty of full and ready supply, of whatever he might expect to obtain in a first-class hotel in any centre. Her furniture and upholstery are of the finest materials, design and finish, at the same time that they can meet the most rigorous demands of sea-service in winter or summer. A thousand persons present in her grand saloons at one time serve only to animate the scene without the least appearance of crowding, and two or three times that number might be "stowed away" within her depths, and the ordinary on-looker would detect no more of bustle or liveliness than is usual in a first-class summering establishment during the height of the season. Here one meets the *elite* of every land. In the grand saloons of an evening the recherche orchestral performances (a feature of this Line) attract audiences representing the wealth and culture and fame of every nation and people, as well as the most popular elements of our own United States society. Seated at the tables in her dining-hall, the most brilliant assemblages of individuals and coteries nightly take place, while the popular features of the situation render perfectly at ease and "at home" the representatives of every respectable walk or station in life. In short, here is to be found Newport, or Cape May, or White Mountain society afloat.

The Bristol and Providence, twin boats of an earlier date than the Pilgrim, and without her iron construction, are yet so nearly of her size that the ordinary eye would never detect that they are a little smaller, while in all essential characteristics of finish, fitting and furnishing the three present no points of difference, excepting occasionally in the color of a decoration or style of ornamentation. Substantially, and for all the purposes for which they are designed, these three steamboats are equally capable, comfortable and safe, nor is there the slightest difference in the manner of their service or its quality. Each has the same number of state-rooms, and all the general and particular features found upon one are repeated in the other. Nevertheless the Pilgrim is slightly the larger craft, and her peculiar construction renders her the superior of any vessel of her class afloat, from a purely

QUARTER DECK OR SMOKING ROOM, STEAMER PILGRIM.

nautical stand-point. The "Old Colony" and "Newport" are lesser boats in size only, the same general system prevailing on all; in fact, the ship's company and the routine may be transferred from one of these boats to another within a few hours' time, as indeed they often are, and not the slightest change be made in the order of things.

In all matters of management and personal service the same high standards are maintained on these boats. A feature is the finely drilled life-saving service, which each boat sustains for itself, and the men composing which have no other duties to perform. Ensconced in their quarters above the paddle wheel, the men of this service stand over their little boat, ready to jump at the least show of any marine accident. A complete and thoroughly drilled fire brigade is also kept in finest organization and practice, every man in each ship's company having his position and duties in case of fire alarm, and being exercised in port during the days, from time to time, to ensure the most perfect readiness for emergencies — which, however, so far as fire alarms are concerned, do not occur twice in a decade. Every nook and corner of the boats are kept with the utmost regard for sanitary and cleanly considerations, and the saloons, state-rooms, cabins, etc., have all the characteristics of a lady's boudoir in these respects, so thorough are their cleansing and renovation every day.

But not alone the quality of the service and the excellent accommodations offered by this Line induce to an experience of its advantages. The route traversed, the trip itself, present superlative attractions, of which even veteran travellers never tire, and which possess peculiar charms and surprises for the novice. These boats leave the pier in New York at a comparatively early hour in the summer afternoons. Before the night "shuts down," from 30 to 40 miles of New York harbor and bay and the Sound will have been traversed, this expanse comprising a series of the most beautiful sights imaginable, and which the world elsewhere cannot equal. The route is down the North and East rivers, skirting miles of the water front of Manhattan (New York city), passing under the Brooklyn Bridge; along the entire length of Blackwell's Island and within biscuit-toss of its shores; through "Hell Gate"; pursuing the tortuous course among the beautiful islands of the lower straits, and finally emerging into the broader waters of Long Island Sound, while the light-houses and light-ships are firing their beacons, which come out one by one on every hand as do the stars in the firmament above and around. The accompaniments of this charming sail are of craft of every size, shape and kind; toiling ships, brigs, schooners, yachts; ponderous ferry-boats; swift-gliding, sharp-bowed excursion steamers and packets; puffing steam-launches and lesser craft; laboring, complaining tugboats, drawing huge burdens of canal boats, flats, rafts, transports, and dumping craft of every name and kind. On the shores are the works of art and institutions of industry or philanthropy or pleasure in countless variety. The fairest landscapes; quaint little nooks and passages and tiny bays running into the land; headlands ornamented or relieved by establishments arising out of the endless devices of man; the most beautiful country-seats and estates; great public institutions; far-reaching vistas and perspectives leading among greenest islets with whitest shores; white and blue and dark green water patches and expanses alternating; glorious old wooded hills coming down to the water's edge at various points; railway trains darting about inland, and visible in the intervals; seabirds circling and screaming overhead; the excitement of meeting and passing craft in narrow channels and passages — who can recount all the attractive features of this magnificent summer trip? And as one views all the details, the great company sitting or standing about upon the steamer's decks is animate with the passing natural stimulation, and description and comment and narration, with the bright jest or witty repartee, fly briskly around, the band meanwhile discoursing choicest music. The gong sounds in every part of the boat, summoning all to the great dining-cabin, which will shortly assume the appearance of a banqueting hall indeed.

Dinner (or supper) over, the concert in the grand saloon is in order, and until 10 o'clock the musical presentations will delight all who feel inclined to their seductive influences. But on the moonlight nights more attractive scenes even than these are offered by the steamer's outer decks. Here, seated with entire comfort, or pacing with true after-dinner abandon, the best realization of a restful, quiet hour may be had. The mixed land and sea breezes, softened and tempered to the most desirable of summer enjoyments, fan the cheek. Even the hum of the great city is past and gone. The moonbeams shimmer on the wavelets, or glance from the white sails of the passing craft, and make long silver pathways towards shores just outlined in the seemingly far distance. The sentinel lights flash up and out at intervals, while the lesser beacons, twinkling from the hulls or rigging of the accompanying vessels, give evidence that darkness brings no suspension of animation upon the water. Fleecy clouds sail overhead, and as these occasionally cross the face of the moon the lights upon and around the Sound waters come out clearer and brighter, and the foamy wake left broad behind the swift-going steamer gleams all the whiter for the change. The Sound grows broader and broader, and the conviction comes more and more forcibly that this night *must* be passed upon the sea.

One of the best and most prized features of the Fall River Line trip is that the passenger may enjoy his bed and night's sleep as completely and securely as on land. The state-rooms of these steamers, roomy, elegant and thoroughly equipped, are full of "downy sleep" for all who commit themselves to their seclusion, and the perfection of night travelling is here to be found. Mosquitos? who ever heard of a mosquito on the Pilgrim, or the Bristol, or the Providence? All that is

STAIRCASE, STEAMER PILGRIM.

required of the cool night breezes may be admitted to the rooms at the will of the occupants, and long before midnight the great ship has settled down to a quiet as profound as that which reigns in the farm-house on the shores a few miles away, while the most careful and vigilant sentinels keep watch and ward in every department, that no unseemly influence shall get the upper hand while mortals sleep.

In the early morning hours Newport and Fall River are reached, and from the last-named point a short 50 miles, by swiftest express train,

takes one to Boston; and matters are so arranged that one of these
trains may be taken and the Hub city reached at 7 o'clock; or breakfast
may be leisurely enjoyed on board the boat, and a supplementary express
reach the city at about 9 o'clock. In either case, the passenger is
left undisturbed in his slumbers to the latest moment, and is not
required to break his rest until the sun has begun a new day's march.
And if one is travelling the other way, or from Boston or Newport to
New York instead of from West to East, then the beautiful sections
of the western Sound and New York Bay and harbor are traversed
in the morning hours—an enchanting trip, indeed. It is always a
beautiful sight to witness morning break over ocean scenes, or situations into which Old Ocean enters be it ever so slightly; but in
these favored localities, where Nature and the arts of man so com-
mingle their influences, who can describe the effects? It is interesting,
too, to note the awakening of a great city like New York; to witness
the throwing off the trammels of the night, the energetic entrance of
the new day, the animated, nimble plunge forward of humanity, as if
to make up for time which had been inadvertently lost. No person can
ever regret the experiences of a trip which contains revelations like
these.

The ministrations of the Fall River Line have reached a higher pitch
of perfection than ever before. To the West and South, as well as to
the communities in the immediate neighborhood, so to speak, of its
New York terminus, it stands the portal to all the glorious summering-
places of South-eastern Massachusetts, as well as to Northern New
England and the East. Nantucket, Martha's Vineyard, Cape Cod,
Plymouth Rock, the South Shore, Onset, the Old Colony—all these
places and sections must be reached by the Old Colony Railroad system,
of which the Fall River Line is the principal adjunct and coadjutor.
The North Shore, the White Mountains, all the eastern New England
coasts, the lake region of Maine, Montreal and Quebec, the splendid
Acadian and Nova Scotian sections—these, too, find in the Fall River
Line their nearest and best connecting highway and point of introduc-
tion. To Newport this Line is the right arm, bringing within its reach
all the necessaries of its life. As a means of communication between
New York and Boston this Line has no equal, and as a transportation
system generally it has no superior on earth. The most rigid examin-
ation or testing of these claims will surely result in their entire justifi-
cation.

NEWPORT.

NEWPORT is one of the famous watering-places of the world. For upwards of two centuries the "Island of Rhodes" has held a reputation universally recognized as being the summering-place *par excellence* of the western hemisphere, while the older civilized countries of the earth can present no localities devoted to the same purposes and pursuits so generously endowed by Nature, or which respond so satisfactorily to the developments and appliances of humanity. In point of mild climatic influences, and situation affording summer conditions prolonged throughout a great portion of the year, some localities lying in the low latitudes on both sides the Atlantic may be rated as superior, when those conditions alone are considered; but with regard to all other features characterizing the place Newport stands alone, and far above and beyond any specimens of combined natural and artificial handiwork displayed anywhere for the admiration of mankind.

Unlike many other localities of which these pages treat, Newport is not now, as it were, introducing to the public notice. Her beauties and facilities and advantages were known to the world long ago, and improvement and occupation, rather than development, have been the order here for many decades past. In a general way Newport has been known and appreciated in every section of the country of which she forms a minute part during many generations, and her dedication was made so long since that she has become one of the permanent institutions of the continent. There are about Newport none of the conditions or attributes of an experiment — an unfinished, partially tested project, which may or may not turn for the better or worse as time progresses, or as human society is affected by whims and fancies. Her establishments and institutions have acquired the permanency of her crags and ledges; and the influences and attractions which inhere in her artificial situation have the same lasting qualities as the natural features which distinguish her, — the shores and their scenes, the outlooks, and the varied presentations of her unrivalled landscapes.

Not that Newport has by any means arrived at the summit of her glories. Constantly all her improvements are enlarging and her advantages entering upon and employing. More than ten years ago her taxable property amounted to upwards of $30,000,000; and the increase during the decade last past has been in a greatly increased ratio over those years which preceded it, so that at the present time much larger figures must be taken to represent the values. A chief peculiarity of Newport lies in the fact that along with the possession of natural attractions superlative in many respects, and many of them to be found nowhere else, she has a permanent population representing wealth and culture such as enters into only the most striking communities of the world, forming an additional or supplementary attraction during the summer months which draws thitherward representatives of its kind from every section, with the result of constantly adding to the value and brilliancy of the establishment already secured, and stimulating to still higher performance efforts long since begun in beautifying, occupying and utilizing all the favored situations of the island. Nowhere else is the beneficent union of the natural and the artificial more observable than in Newport; and it may readily be discovered here how much the one depends upon the other of these conditions, and how greatly the quality of each is enhanced by its existence in connection with the other.

Premising, that which is the exact truth, that Newport is a fashionable resort, as well as an object of pilgrimage for thousands of people from every walk in life, it may be well to trace some of its principal attractions, and thus to obtain some appreciation of its advantages

CLIFF WALK, NEWPORT.

and claims to consideration, which may assist in a worthy estimate of its importance. And first with regard to historical features : —

The island was first purchased from the native Indian owners in 1638, comparatively only a short time, as will be seen, after the landing of the Pilgrim Fathers at Plymouth. The original name of the locality was "Aquidneck," signifying "Isle of Peace," itself a significant title, bestowed on account of real qualities so apparent that even the Indian proprietors could not but recognize their existence. Not long after this purchase the locality received the name of the "Isle of Rhodes," on account of the near resemblance to its namesake in the Mediterranean Sea. During the greater part of the Revolutionary War the place was occupied by the British, the foreign armies encamping on its beautiful sites during the summer months, and forcing themselves into the houses of the inhabitants in winter. As usual with these forces, wherever in this country they could "make their mark," during the war above referred to, they destroyed or sadly mutilated all the creations of the place which came within their power during their occupancy; and without doubt they would gladly have ruined beyond redemption all the natural features also, could they have done this before they were compelled to evacuate. During their stay the Newport waters were always occupied by their vessels of war, and many of these were finally burned when the French fleet appeared off the coasts, and the British were preparing to "cut and run," six war ships being given to the flames, besides other small cruisers, two galleys blown up, fifteen large transports sunk in the outer harbor, and other war vessels sunk in the neighborhood, while a sloop-of-war and thirty armed vessels were sunk in the inner harbor. The summer sojourner, enjoying from the beach or some grassy or rocky outlook near the shore, the beautiful ocean display spread out before him, is sure to look upon an expanse which upwards of a century ago was made animate by the presence and movements of the hostile fleet above referred to, the officers and men of which were pestilent vandals, overrunning all the section about them, and desirous only of working ruin and desolation upon all around. In 1779 the British forces evacuated, the population of the town having decreased from 12,000 to 4,000 during their stay; and the commercial interests of the place had received a blow from which they never recovered.

Newport was a patriot rendezvous and a celebrated naval station even in the old Colonial times. Before the Revolutionary War fortifications had been erected upon its localities, and Fort Adams, now so prominent and so fine a feature in its belongings, was begun in 1814, and exists one of the most important of United States coast defences, fitted to mount 468 guns and garrison 3,000 men. The remains of the older forts and the full establishment of the more recent are part of the Newport treasures, and may be examined at leisure by her summer visitors, the army and naval establishments of the place contributing very much to the interest and attractions of this centre. Government has also made this a scientific headquarters in sundry departments, and always may be found here various corps of official representatives, adding lustre to the social attractions of the place, as well as contributing greatly to the interests which multiply here. Thus this beautiful island is sought out and included in the visitations of the scientific, military, naval and historic, as well as social and literary representatives of every civilized nation, who find here all sorts of attractions and advantages mingled, and who by their presence at all seasons, and especially in summer time, render the situation brilliant with varied charms.

Newport was the home of Commodore Perry, and here his monument stands, a principal, as it is an honored, feature of the attractions of the place. Here Gen. Washington was entertained by Count Rochambeau, after the arrival of the French fleet and during the War of the Revolution; and here in the old State House is the magnificent picture of the "Father of his Country," painted by Stuart and presented by

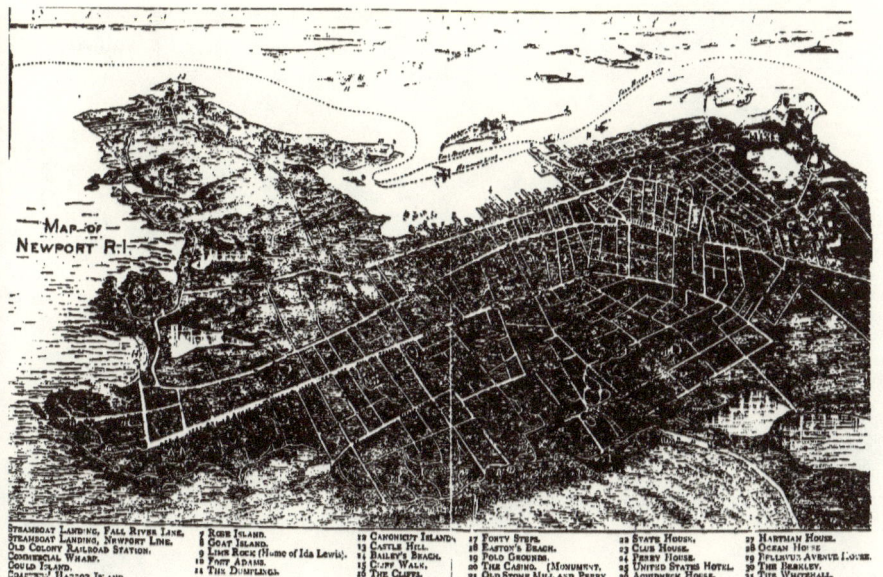

MAP OF
NEWPORT R.I.

STEAMBOAT LANDING, FALL RIVER LINE.   7 ROSE ISLAND.   12 CANONICUT ISLAND.   17 FORTY STEPS.   22 STATE HOUSE.   27 HARTMAN HOUSE.
STEAMBOAT LANDING, NEWPORT LINE.   8 GOAT ISLAND.   13 CASTLE HILL.   18 EASTON'S BEACH.   23 CLUB HOUSE.   28 OCEAN HOUSE.
OLD COLONY RAILROAD STATION.   9 LIME ROCK (Home of Ida Lewis). 14 BAILEY'S BEACH. 19 POLO GROUNDS.   24 PERRY HOUSE.   29 BELLEVUE AVENUE HOUSE.
COMMERCIAL WHARF.   10 FORT ADAMS.   15 CLIFF WALK.   20 THE CASINO. (MONUMENT.   25 UNITED STATES HOTEL.   30 THE BERKLEY.
GOULD ISLAND.   11 THE DUMPLINGS.   16 THE CLIFFS.   21 OLD STONE MILL AND PERRY   26 AQUIDNECK HOUSE.   31 THE WHITEHALL.
COASTERS' HARBOR ISLAND.

beau, after the arrival of the French fleet and during the War of the
Revolution; and here in the old State House is the magnificent picture
of the "Father of his Country," painted by Stuart and presented by

that artist to the town. Here is the famous old "Stone Mill," the Round Tower of the Norsemen, whose existence has furnished material for endless researches and disquisitions on the part of historical societies and individuals, and has attracted and induced investigation by savants of every name and period for many generations; and in Newport are some of the famous libraries of the country, the "Redwood" having been established here in the middle of the last century. A century and a quarter ago there were upwards of seventy Jewish families residing in Newport, and their members were among the most wealthy and influential of the island's population. The Jewish synagogue and cemetery still remaining, and various monuments scattered about the place, to this day attest the value and importance of this element in the affairs of the ancient town. Numerous church edifices and dwellings of historic significance are to be found on every hand, and these are connected in so many ways with eminent ancient names and associations, that the Newport visitor will find a rich mine of research opened to his inspection, if he is in any degree interested in the worthy past of this country and her enactments.

The historic associations connected with "Tammany (Miantonomi) Hill," once the seat of government of the Indian sachems, will also be found intensely interesting. During the Revolution this hill was surmounted by breastworks of British creation, and the direction of these, with something of their conformation, may still be traced. On one side of this hill stood once the famous "Malbone House," and some of the finest outlooks possible to Newport are from its neighborhoods.

Newport's art and artistic history are also noticeable features. Besides the Stuart picture alluded to above, and the artist Stuart himself, numerous distinguished artists have been associated at different periods here, and their connections with the place are of significant interest. Smilert painted here, and Samuel King was a portrait painter in the town, and the store No. 130 Thames Street furnished the asylum wherein Malbone and Allston were instructed by this artist in the rudiments of their art. There are also some Stuart pictures in the Redwood Library. In a not inferior sense Newport may claim to be the cradle of the art of the country, for here at early periods some of the most enthusiastic and determined votaries of the calling lived and toiled and endured.

But great as are the historic charms and associations of this favored locality, they take vastly inferior place when compared with the natural and featural attractions of the island. Here are to be found absolutely all the requisites which must or may enter into the constitution of a complete seashore "watering-place," and all the elements are of a quality unrivalled elsewhere in existence. The landscapes, the unrivalled water-views, the magnificent shores lying between the two — what bit of country elsewhere can equal these? The breezes which perpetually play over this locality possess the peculiar invigorating

VIEWS AT NEWPORT R. I.

qualities which distinguish all the shore situations of south-eastern Massachusetts and New England, and their life and health-giving properties have more than once been alluded to in these pages. The immense water surface surrounding the place, renovating and purifying by ceaseless movement, ensures a constant succession of cool air currents, disposing to sleep among the summer heats, and providing for soundest slumbers under any reasonable circumstances. There is nothing pent-up or confined about the Newport situation. One may wander for miles, and ride or walk for hours together, with no natural reminder that there are limits to the situation; indeed, in summer, here is an apparent Paradise without bounds. The land surface is undulating, carpeted in season with brightest verdure and vegetable growth; the shores are alternate beaches and ledges, overhung with white cliffs or brown crags, or gently sloping backward and upward into greenest pastures or intervales. The surrounding islands are gems in fairest ocean setting, inviting to summer delights and quiet, restful influences. The headlands and rock-strewn points render even the ocean storms delightful and attractive, and illustrate the grandeur and the energy of the watery wastes as no other creations can do. And the waters themselves — what language can describe their myriad fascinations, or pen-pictures illustrate their marvellous manifestations?

A drive-way now extends entirely around the Newport shores, following the conformation of the coast, winding over hill and headland and through plains and dells, now affording from the summit of some bold elevation an outlook over miles of ocean scenes, and at times narrowing the gaze within the limits of fairest island shores, or about some sheltered cove or nook, a perfect nest of summer beauties. Now the surf rolls grandly almost to the very carriage side, and anon the white beach gleams far below, spread out with its throngs of animate and inanimate existence like the enchanting fancied views of artistic creation. This road extends for many miles, and includes in its circuit all the varieties of Newport scenery and surroundings. The harbor, the bay, the roadstead, the ocean — all in turn present their wonderful attributes and features; and the succession of beauties would be surfeiting, were it not that Nature overwhelms without bewildering. Imposing beyond expression are these scenes, and they are not to be understood or appreciated at a single view or experience. They are wonderful studies, and present ever new details as a reward to the interested observer. There is no danger of satiating or tiring in their presence, if one has any element of soundness in his mental or physical make-up.

The harbor presents views of constant activity, with pictures of every form of artificial marine life imaginable. Here are representatives of all manner of gallant shipping, from the stately man-of-war to the white-winged yacht and its miniature attendant — the "pumpkin-seed" dingey. The little, puffing tugboat or steam-launch cuts the water surface alongside such steam leviathans as the "Pilgrim" and her associates of the Fall River Line; and all find their home in these beautiful waters, and naturally play their parts therein. The boats of all the clubs and squadrons known to fame, and of many important only in the estimation of their immediate associates, alternately rendezvous here, — the Puritans and Genestas and Americas of the fancy navies of the world; and new and untried specimens of marine architecture or contrivance make their first experiments from this haven. Here some of the most significant ocean performances known to history have received their initial movement; and in the realm of romance Newport waters and shores have furnished abundant location for the most fascinating revelations.

A peculiar charm of Newport waters is the alternative of pretty,

BOAT-HOUSE LANDING, NEWPORT.

land-locked bays and harbors of the most placid and mirror-like surfaces, with ocean rolling in majesty and dashing against crags and along iron-bound ledges and reefs. Few localities present these features so completely, or upon so grand a scale. The scenes are not all in miniature, but of the fullest and most perfect significance imaginable. At Graves' Point, Brenton's Reef, Purgatory, or Spouting Rock, or along any part of the eastern shore, no beholder will ever make the mistake of supposing he is taking in a contracted view of Old Ocean.

Of course, there is afforded here on all sides the finest opportunities for boating of every kind, and fishing-grounds in great variety offer on every hand. There are within the Newport territory many fresh water sheets in which are found perch and other varieties of the fish which inhabit such homes, while in the ocean waters around may be caught those kinds which have become famous either for their "gamey" qualities, which commend them so highly to the average mortal, or for their edible attributes, or both combined, as in the case of the bluefish, bass, etc. Not at all to be despised is the sport of following with well-sharpened grainse or "iron," the porpoise or swordfish shoals, which afford not only the rarest hunting, but juicy bits of sea-meat, astonishing to the palate of the novice in marine cuisine.

This little volume is not a guide-book, and it would be impossible within its pages and scope to present in detail the attractions or the localities of Newport and its surroundings, or, indeed, of any of the sections enumerated in its Table of Contents. Brenton's Reef, with its rocky waste extending a mile out from the shore into the sea, and over which the waves continually break and tumble and roar; Spouting Rock, with its mysterious caverns, where, when the great ocean storms are on, the waters madly plunge and rush and dash into myriad fragments, and rise in great jets skyward through the "horn;" "Purgatory," that yawning gulf, the scene of countless legends and traditions, and the actual repository of secrets which the scientist is forever striving to unravel; the "Flints;" "Hobson's Hole;" "Coggeshall Ledge;" "The Dumplings;" "Green End;" — will not these and a thousand other charming or wonderful situations become familiar to the sojourner who tempts Newport influences? Even so — and the half cannot be told!

And although in her "make-up" Newport associates the summer homes of the Vanderbilts, Lorrillards, Belmonts, Astors, and countless other names representing distinguishing qualities of wealth or culture or well-known deeds, grand caravansaries fitted to entertain the "lords of the earth," and the establishments and appliances of luxury and elegant leisure, she invites equally the humblest summer sojourner or recreation-seeker, and knows no partiality in the provision made for all to partake of her peculiar delights. Her summer-houses, public and private, are equally open to every respectable comer, and the institutions above alluded to are at the service of all who care to profit by or avail themselves of the provisions. The great steamers of the Fall River Line, which make regular landing here, are loaded through the entire season with delegations of the popular hosts which call the United States their country, as well as by the fortune-favored representatives, who indulge every whim and taste of which they may become possessed, and wander up and down upon the earth at will. The trains of the Old Colony Railroad system bring to this locality daily throughout the summer great throngs from every part of New England and the North; and never a soul among them all fails of a welcome in the ancient Newport town. This place long since learned how best to provide and care for summer visitors. It is the business of the place to show its good qualities, and these are all in the direction of making summer delightful.

NANTASKET AND ITS NEIGHBORHOOD.

ALMOST immediately upon leaving the South Boston station of the Old Colony Railroad the features which make this road famous as a seashore line begin to become apparent. Long before the territory of Boston has been left behind, the passenger finds himself skirting the shores of Dorchester Bay, with Dorchester Heights (South Boston), a succession of most attractive islands, numerous points and headlands, and the outspread waters of the bay in full view from car windows. Ten miles out, and upon leaving the Braintree station, the line bears away eastward and trends toward the famous South Shore, always a most magnetic attraction for summer tourists and sojourners. Passing the station in ancient Hingham, a connecting branch of the Old Colony a mile or two below leaves the main line, and changing course abruptly within a few minutes brings the passenger upon the sands of Nantasket.

Nantasket, with its beach and surroundings, has often been called the " Coney Island of Boston." Nantasket Beach has become celebrated as one of the finest ocean shores on the United States coast, presenting as it does more of the elements which make up the grand, the attractive, and the complete in border scenery than are often found combined. The surf, pouring inward from the expanse of a great ocean and washing a beach of clearest sands, which glitter in the summer sun-rays and send back in myriad flashing streams the water which never ceases thus to advance and retreat; the enclosing hills, ragged and craggy, with projecting rock-masses upon one side and evenly rounded and verdure-clad upon the other; the endless panorama of life upon the water, constantly in motion and ever-changing in the view; the great ships, cloud-enveloped steamers, and the accompaniment of the lesser variety of the products of naval skill and architecture; the rolling porpoise and the snorting, spouting puffer or finback enlivening the outlook; the light-houses and beacons alternating upon headland, or shoal, or island ledge; all these and many other attractions are found at Nantasket, to say nothing of cool, invigorating breezes, and the proximity to centres which renders its location within such easy reach that its denizens may, within the hour, find themselves in a new atmosphere — a new world, in fact.

The beach is dotted with hotels, varying in pretensions from the humble lunch or restaurant establishment to the lordly caravansary, vieing in table, service and accommodations with the best in the land, and especially designed and kept for the purposes they are to serve — that is, for summer guests and sojourners. Multitudes of children

come here, and disport with perfect safety and the most beneficial
results in the light-curling surf, the water being of excellent temperature for bathing purposes. At the far west end of the beach are the
clustering highlands and headlands in the midst of which reposes Hull,
with its outlying summer cottages dotting the hill-sides, its noble hostelries, and most congenial and domestic habitues. Windmill Point, or
Point Pemberton, with its great modern hotel, tips the whole; and
around this point sweep the fleet, the puffing steamers, and anon the
fishers' boats, rendering the scene always animated, and continually
renewing its features.

In summer time this beach for its entire length is constantly alive,
not alone with the tourists and visitors who make short pilgrimages to

its sands, but with dwellers and campers who establish headquarters
here, and pass the whole season among its delights. So near the city
is it that one may ensconce himself in any of the great hotels for
which Boston is famous, and still spend two-thirds of the time in the
Nantasket neighborhood, the evenings being if anything even more
interesting than the days in this locality. But the local hotels and
private establishments of the place afford every imaginable facility and
accommodation for sojourners, and congenial company, as well as the
most varied entertainment, is sure to be met with on all sides.

Next to the sanitary advantages, a principal element in the make-up
of the Nantasket region as a summering-place is found in its glorious

outlooks. The Nantasket beach, or headland, projects far inward among the islands which dot the mouth of Boston Harbor, and which are justly ranked with the most beautiful island groups of the American coast. In full view from almost any part of this section is the harbor, the roadstead, and the broad opening into Massachusetts Bay, with all the variety of animate and inanimate existence which distinguishes these localities. Looking westward, glimpses of charming water surfaces, vistas and perspectives of the Dorchester Bay sheet, are afforded through the island formations; and these change like the figures in a kaleidoscope with every shifting stand-point. Northward the Brewsters, the Graves, Calf Island, and a dozen lesser islets, bound the immediate view, with the roadstead rolling between always animate with shipping and the inhabitants of the air and water. Away beyond these islands is the "North Shore," fair to look upon in every part in summer, and daintily colored by the constantly changing influences of the sea and air around, presenting a picture which no artist can copy, so grand are its effects and so perfect its combinations, while the attractions are varied with every passing cloud or refracting mist from the water surface. Eastward, the long swell of the Atlantic shows in the heaving, swelling face of the great bay, while near at hand are the rock-bound shores of Cohasset, the huge rocks lifting their iron-grey backs above the surface of the water at intervals, in the fair days appearing like basking leviathans taking their rest; but during the ocean storms they check the maddened waters and send them flying skyward in great, feathering masses, while all around their bases the white-gleaming breakers beat wildly, and the billows rush and roar and swallow up each other with ten thousand times the force of giants in battle. Nowhere on the United States coasts can an ocean storm be witnessed under such advantageous circumstances as in the Cohasset neighborhood; and one who has looked upon Old Ocean in his majesty during a "north-easter," as experienced from these stand-points, has learned something of the forces of Nature, and witnessed her tragic performances, in a theatre whose resources are grand beyond the power of man to describe.

Out of the rock-bed, and seemingly out of the midst of the sea, rises the sentinel tower of Minot's Ledge; and other famous light establishments are visible on every hand. Below Nantasket, Green Hill rises, and a succession of delightful localities along the shore or immediately inland lie between the beach and the Cohasset territory, the undulating, tree-grown hill-sides more than half concealing the most beautiful driveways which, like the "Jerusalem Road," have attracted to their vicinity wealthy and cultured dwellers, who have planted most luxurious summering establishments, and turned the region into a repository of artistic and like associations, as well as of the choicest natural beauties and attractions.

Looking southward from the beach, the islands, headlands, and main between which lie spread out enchanting bits of water scenery, stretch away inland to the Hingham, Weymouth and Quincy shores; and winding in and about, following the tortuous channels or the deeper waters of the place, every variety of small craft may constantly be seen. The white tents of camping-parties dot the green hill-sides around, while grey old boulders and rock-patches, with their coadjutors the members of the dark fir tribe, lend enough of sombre coloring to relieve the otherwise excessive brightness of the summer hues in this section. Viewed from the summits or sides of Sagamore or Strawberry hills, which rise out of the Nantasket sands as though planned naturally as stand-points for outlooks, or from the Allerton headland, how grand the views on every side from this Queen of sea beaches!

A transportation line — the "Nantasket Beach Railroad" — runs from the Old Colony House station on the South Shore Branch of the Old Colony Railroad to the extreme point — Point Pemberton — of Nantasket Beach, appearing a backbone for the locality. From the windows of its moving trains most wonderful outlooks upon every side are afforded; and as these views include great water surfaces and their surroundings, with much that is going forward upon them, the usual objection made to the scenic accompaniments of railroad travelling, viz., that the glimpses are fleeting and very imperfect, will not hold in this section.

This whole region has historic associations of no mean order. Across the bay, inland from Nantasket, and easily reached by sailboat threading the most delightful water-paths among the islands and headlands, in the old Quincy township, is the site of "Merry Mount." It was here that "Morton and his ungodly crew," the degenerate offshoots who caused the Pilgrim Fathers so much trouble and anxiety, held high carnival; and their orgies at Merry Mount and Nantasket — for the Pilgrims considered their diversions as nothing better than orgies — often included both the nights and days of their existence, and illustrated every phase of human enjoyments, except, perhaps, the highest and noblest. One cannot help thinking, however, that Morton and his companions selected from the fittest when they adopted this beautiful section as their haunting-places; for even at that early day, and many decades before the region became thickly settled in any part, its natural endowments must have rendered it peculiarly attractive. That it has been a centre of summer delights for upwards of two and a half centuries, and is in that respect the oldest "institution" of its kind (watering-place) in the country, is a fact which may excite investigation as to its claims and attributes; and such investigation, if made in person, never fails to convince.

From the head of Nantasket Beach eastward to the bay shores of Cohasset, including a section four or five miles in length by about as many inland, the character of the formation is entirely changed, as has already been hinted. The shores of Cohasset are magnificent crags or ledges, the latter often running off into the waters of the bay, or uniting with those which rear their forms beyond the surf-line outward.

Its lands stretching backward from the coasts are tumbled about in fantastic hill and cliff formations, enclosing vales and meadows of surpassing loveliness, over which the rarest tempered breezes blow, and which are excellent centres of dairy and farming operations. This union of hill and dale with the magnificent ocean scenery, and the unequalled sanitary advantages of the section, has attracted from time to time people of discernment and means, who have located their summer estates or cottages within or about the Cohasset or Hingham villages, from whence all the facilities and provisions of the region are made available. The little collection of contiguous estates on the eastern side of Cohasset (at "The Point," overlooking the harbor), belonging to the actors Lawrence Barrett, Robson and Crane, furnish an illustration of the situation. There is, however, nothing of crowding in the region. Inland the scenes are rural and simple, though qualified by oft-repeated

instances of the presence of the votaries of art and cultivation, while great patches of country, and the shores from "end to end," remain just as they came fresh from the hand of the Creator, with all the majesty and grandeur of their first formation, and neither belittled or intruded upon by the innovations of humanity. In the late Fall the Cohasset shores become the resort of a class of sportsmen, members of whom often travel great distances to attain this rendezvous and the excitements and pleasures of coot-shooting. Cohasset forms the northerly limit of the area furnished by the Massachusetts coasts for this sporting, the other extreme being found in South Plymouth, while all the intermediate shores — the Scituates, Marshfield, etc., — are included in the "field." These Fall visitors, besides unlimited indulgence in the sport they so much affect, also secure a season of communion with Old Ocean and his dependencies especially significant and attractive; for there are elements and conditions present during these weeks of the dying year peculiar to the region, and highly prized by lovers of Nature who also appreciate her more rugged moods and presentations. Every year the number of those who prolong their stay about this seashore section increases; and there are diversions and pastimes belonging to the late season regarding which only experimental knowledge is of any account.

Hingham village is a repetition of Cohasset without the rocky and surf-beaten shores of the last-named. Its water front is connected with the placid and untroubled waters of the inland bays, and the peculiar formation of Nantasket and the neighboring shores protects it from the energy and fury of the Atlantic billows. Nevertheless, all its advantages are those of a first-class ocean watering-place, and its connection with the near city in summer is equally certain and expeditious by land or water transportation. Among its local features is to be found one of the finest rural cemeteries in the country, holding within its bosom the ashes of some of the most illustrious dead of Massachusetts. As things go in this country, Hingham is indeed an "ancient" town; but the references to antiquity most noticeable here by the tourist or sojourner are rather in the direction of honorable families and family names, historic associations, and the preservation of grand old manners and customs, than to "old style" buildings, monuments or observances. As a summering-place its excellences of every sort are of the highest order; while the health-seeker, or worn-out mortal, to whom absolute rest must prove the best boon earth can afford, may find all desires gratified here, with such air and sunshine and recreative influences "thrown in" as he has little dreamed of. For boating and driving, the coast of New England furnishes but few equals to Hingham, while the peculiar formation and situation of its surrounding hills render it the natural home of campers.

South-westward from Hingham and adjoining it in this direction is Weymouth, one of the great shoe centres of the section; a town of large and irregularly laid-out territory which contains many beautiful locations, and has an inland water-front afforded by deep indentation of the shore line. This place, like most of its neighboring parishes, derives interest apart from its fine natural features through its historic associations. It was here, during the fit of excited feeling which succeeded his ineffectual wooing by deputy, that Myles Standish, the generalissimo of the Pilgrim band, had his famous encounter with the Indian chiefs, which added more to his reputation for prowess than to the general regard for his humanitarian principles. Longfellow has pictured the event and its climax in his usual vivid style. The Indian encampment reached by Standish and his companions (1623), after a three days' march from Plymouth, was

"Pitched on the head of a meadow between the sea and the forest;"

where since that time many a fair encampment has taken place, in which the pleasures of peace and good will, and not the passions of men at war, have proved the charm. Capt. Standish met here the two chiefs Wattawamat and Pecksuot, Indians who hated himself and the whole company of Pilgrim invaders, and would gladly have exterminated them. The savages had not yet much familiarity with fire-arms, and the chiefs demanded largesse of blankets and knives, with more than a hint that muskets and powder would be still more acceptable. Upon being contemptuously turned away by Standish with the offer of nothing but bibles, Wattawamat sprung forth with a bound, shouting:

> "Who is there here to fight with the brave Wattawamat?"
> Then he unsheathed his knife, and, whetting the blade on his left hand,
> Held it aloft, and displayed a woman's face on the handle,
> Saying, with bitter expression and look of sinister meaning,
> 'I have another at home, with the face of a man on the handle.
> By and by they shall marry; and there will be plenty of children!'

> Then stood Pecksuot forth, self-vaunting, insulting Myles Standish;
> While with his fingers he patted the knife that hung at his bosom,
> Drawing it half from its sheath, and plunging it back, as he muttered,
> 'By and by it shall see; it shall eat; ah, ah! but shall speak not!
> This is the mighty Captain the white men have sent to destroy us!
> He is a little man; let him go and work with the women!'"

Meanwhile, Standish—

> "When he heard their defiance, the boast, the taunt and the insult,
> All the hot blood of his race, of Sir Hugh and of Thurston de Standish,
> Boiled and beat in his heart, and swelled in the veins of his temples.
> Headlong he leaped on the boaster, and snatching his knife from its scabbard,
> Plunged it into his heart, and, reeling backwards, the savage
> Fell with his face to the sky, and a fiend-like fierceness upon it."

And at the same time Wattawamat "bit the dust," despatched by a bullet which passed swift through his brain.

Passing fair were the spots of earth upon which these scenes were enacted so many years ago; but no less fair and winsome are they at the present day, when their attractions are enhanced by the myriad inventions and arts of humanity, through which they have been transformed into homes and haunts of surpassing loveliness, and such sojourning places for summer wanderers as are rarely found on earth.

THE SOUTH SHORE.

HE locality known as the "South Shore" begins with the Cohasset coasts and skirts the south-western waters of Massachusetts Bay from these points away round to Plymouth. Within its limits are included the territory of Cohasset, Scituate (North and South), Marshfield, Duxbury and Kingston. Scituate, Marshfield and Duxbury are divided into numerous villages and hamlets, "strung along" the shore, as it were, and presenting at every point the peculiar New England characteristics, with many qualities inherent to the "good Old Colony times," and descended from the same. Overlooking the bay above named, and very nearly opposite the inner shores of Cape Cod, which are distant scarcely more than twenty to twenty-five miles, and in full view under favorable circumstances, this locality partakes to a remarkable degree of the advantages and facilities for seashore "summering" afforded by the region of which it forms a part, and holds some of these excellences in high development. The coasts are an alternation of sand-beach and rock-masses; of slightly curving surf-line, extending sometimes for miles, and broken, indented barriers, marking bold incursions inland of the restless water and the inroads for centuries of angry waves, which have diminished in their unceasing action alike the rugged rocks and the towering cliffs of sand. The billows of the ocean find no check as they roll upon these shores, save in the northern portions, where terrific ledges of iron-grey rocks stand off-shore as natural breakwaters to take the first shock of the elements. The coast-line is clearly defined and easily reached; and the white sails of passing vessels, the monotonously waving wings of the great sea-birds, and the never-ceasing roll and swell and intoning of Old Ocean, renders the scene presented in every part of this section one of constant animation.

City denizens some time since found out the natural attractions of the South Shore as a watering-place, and of late years the summer visitation in all parts here has been of rapid and widely extended growth. The health-giving breezes, the unrivalled facilities afforded for bay fishing (to which reference will be made further on in this book), the peaceful quiet and restful influences of all its neighborhoods, and the entire absence of conventionalities or conditions which require the sojourner to continue irksome society customs or relations, render the section much sought after by wanderers from every part of the country, and present opportunities and inducements for a prolonged indulgence in the *dolce far niente*, irresistible especially by city representatives or travellers from inland homes. Here may come women and children with an absolute certainty of revelling in natural delights which are at the same time safely and profitably experienced; and the extraordinary vanishing of all cares and anxieties is a peculiarity at once observable to every traveller under roof or tent-fly during summer on the South Shore.

The villages are of the quaint, quiet, New England (and especially Massachusetts) sort, well-ordered, tastefully built and kept, and superior in neatness and attention to sanitary details. The invigorating, life-giving, natural qualities of the section are thus seconded by the institutions and practices of its humanity, and comfort and enjoyment here does not in the least depend upon the ministrations of great caravansaries or many-roomed popular hotels, flaunting all the latest and "first-class" attachments. The enjoyments are simply of natural beauties and creations, which are indeed lavishly bestowed; but these are seconded by ample provision for civilized, even cultured humanity in all reasonable and appropriate directions, and the true lover of Nature's grandest offerings and the attributes which have been partially set forth above, will find no disappointment in all this region.

The historic associations belong chiefly to Old Colony periods, and the connections are rather with grand old names and individual or family characters than with remarkable deeds and incidents, though the latter have been by no means left out of South Shore experiences in the past. Not alone the unsophisticated or inexperienced admirer of, or sympathizer with, Dame Nature has found attractions in this neighborhood. Thoreau delighted in these shores, and pronounced the bathing afforded in the vicinity of the great ledges superior to any within his knowledge. "The smooth and fantastically worn rocks, and the perfectly clean and tress-like rock-weeds falling over you, and attached so firmly to the rocks that you could pull yourself up by them, greatly enhanced the luxury of the bath," he writes, and thousands have sympathized with him in this regard. Also he delighted in the long-drawn beaches and the variety of research they suggested and invited, the unique specimens they contributed, the wonderful outlooks they afforded. For the same reasons, doubtless, that so attracted this philosopher to the Cape Cod shores, he became enthusiastic over the section describing. Poets have found inspiration here, and that of the noblest quality.

On a slightly inclined side-hill of one of the Scituate villages, in full view of the shore and the marvellous outstretched waters of the bay beyond, though at some little distance inland from these features, still stands the house and the old well which furnished the material for the construction of "The Old Oaken Bucket," a composition which still in song and recitation moves the family circle in every hamlet from Maine to Mexico, and which has been parodied and imitated in more forms than the ancient bucket can bring up drops at a single excursion of its "sweep."

Nothing more distinguishes the south-eastern coast of Massachusetts than its magnificent, almost unique, provision of the purest water, which leaping from fountains, bubbling in springs, or drawn from cool, caverned depths, delights indeed the palate and the very soul of humanity as only Nature's best productions can. Woodworth's old well, the "Pilgrim Spring" in Plymouth, and a hundred other water-springs in the region, made famous first upon the representations of the ancient Indian owners of the territory, and after by the testimonies and eulogies of their successors, have long since settled matters in this direction.

It will be remembered, too, that Marshfield was the home of Daniel Webster. Here he lived, during the vacations from his duties at the capital city of the country, and here he died and lies buried. The "Webster Place" is still an historic attraction, and the haunts of the great lawyer and statesman are sought out and made familiar to countless tourists and sojourners, who reach these points during the summer season. Mr. Webster had a rare appreciation of the beautiful and harmonious in Nature, and his love for his old Marshfield and Plymouth associations amounted almost to a passion. He knew equally well the best "fish days," whether the game was to be sought in ocean depths, or pond or lakelet. None knew better than he the "ledges" of the bay and how to reach them, or could calculate with more perfect accuracy upon the results of his expeditions. With all the walks and drives, the boulders on the shores, the "short cuts" and the fairest outlooks, he was as familiar as his favorite henchman; and whether the wind "blew high or low," or duties and troubles pressed lightly or heavily, he loved old Marshfield and his seashore home supremely.

The same undulating formation of land which distinguishes the inland territory of Hingham and Cohasset prevails along the whole South Shore; but not all the grounds are so valuable as those of Marshfield, or afford so good facilities for farming or gardening purposes. The communities and situations are thoroughly rural, the population scattered, and the dwellings and hamlets usually occupy sites retired somewhat from the immediate shore. But great colonies assemble on the shores about Brandt Rock and at other points during the warm months, while the facilities for all possible comers and for every reasonable demand of sojourners are on every hand or easily secured. Nearly all the Irish moss of commerce is collected along the South Shore, and the industry fostered by its gathering gives to the section an animated feature which must count among its attractions. The Scituate shores are crowned with frowning sand cliffs, as well known to the cruisers of the bay, or to navigators from foreign parts as is "Minot's," or the Great Brewster. Along the Marshfield coast great wooded hills occupy instead of sand cliffs; and these are multiplied until almost profusion in this direction is reached in Duxbury, once the military headquarters of the Old Colony. From these elevations of every kind the most magnificent outlooks reward all comers; and one may sit for hours without tiring upon these upheavals, scanning the waters with their shifting panorama, or giving way to the influences of air and sunshine while these work magic renewal in worn-out frames. Especially grand

are the scenes as viewed from Duxbury, whose visions include, besides the bay and its surroundings, the whole expanse of Plymouth harbor and its environs, as well as its own lovely shores and characteristic landscapes.

And all this region, too, is specially favored by the Old Colony Railroad train service during the summer months. Communication with the cities and the inland centres is constant and perfect, so that it may be made available upon the slightest press of need; and yet the sojourner in any part here is as much isolated in fact from the outside world as though he were beyond its reach and hearing, as well as its sight. In all these localities one may breakfast of a morning upon ocean fish of his own catching, and sup with a friend or congenial party in New York, Saratoga, or the White Mountains upon the same day. He may busy himself and live like a hermit, or an ancient fisherman, for days or weeks together if he will; or indulge in a round of visitation or touring from these headquarters which shall include every section of coast from Nova Scotia to New Jersey, and all the mountain and lake resorts in New England,—and their name is Legion. Is not this the perfection of summering?

PLYMOUTH.

T HE historic associations connected with Plymouth would render the town an object of veneration and pilgrimage, aside from any of the usual considerations through which certain localities are popularized as watering-places. But whoever supposes — and thousands have heretofore made the mistake — that this ancient town depends alone upon its historic connection for the element of attractiveness, stands in need of enlightenment. Indeed, no situation on the entire Massachusetts coast presents so many and varied features which go to make up the ideal summering-place; for here both land and water combine to furnish pleasures, diversions, recreative employments, scenery and associations, surpassingly full in every department and superlative in lavishness and quality.

The territory of Plymouth is irregular in "lay out," the town being eighteen miles long and from four to nine miles wide, the coast-line including, as the result of numerous indentations and tortuous windings, nearly double the length above mentioned. For physical features, the land is broken in outline and rolling in every part, being heaped up in quick succeeding hills and ranges, like the billows of the ocean in a strong tideway, this conformation affording situation for numerous ponds and lakelets, hundreds of which are to be found within the town limits, their clear waters, usually white-sanded shores and bottoms, and surroundings of venerable wood-growth, rendering them most attractive features, to say nothing of the stores of fine fish with which many of them are stocked, either naturally or by artificial method. The forests are ancient and primeval, sometimes extending for miles without a break save where great fires have devastated, and showing neither building or clearing in evidence that man ever brought the region under subjection. Within the past decade as many as 200 deer have been killed in these and the adjacent woods of Sandwich during a single year, and not a season passes that sportsmen or sojourners do not see specimens of this noble game in these locations. Skirting the lakes and ponds and winding over and among the hills, innumerable roads thread, well-defined and hardened by the usage of nearly three centuries, and affording the most beautiful driveways imaginable. Delightsome ocean views are obtained from the summits of hill-tops extending for miles inland, and outlooks over fair sections of hill and dale, with water-bits shimmering and glistening in the picture, so beautiful that sometimes the original Indian occupants of the land bestowed their most musically descriptive names to designate the sections or localities. Springs of purest water abound and bubble over on every

side, often proving the sources of the finest ponds; or, starting out
from the hill-sides, run away in merry streams to outlets upon lake or
ocean shore. Among these scenes Daniel Webster revelled for days in
succession, accompanied by a few choice friends, never forgetting the
Natty Bumppo of the region, and varying the divertisements by visits
to well-known fishing-grounds in the bay near by.

And where can be found ocean-shores, or ocean-views, or any of the
delights that the salt sea can afford when contiguous to the land,
superior to the natural provision which distinguishes Plymouth and
her surroundings? There are beaches of hardest and whitest sand, the
shores in places exposed to the ceaseless rolling of the surf, and again
receiving the advances of the tides quietly, without the turning of
a single tiny sand-crystal. From the rock which marks the landing-
place of the Pilgrim Fathers away round to the "White Horse," beyond
Manomet and Indian Hill to Sandwich line, isolated boulders, rock-
patches and masses and craggy formations alternate, realizing with

every increase of the ocean breezes the ideal which haunted the mind
of the poetess when she wrote : —

> " The breaking waves dashed high
> On a stern and rock-bound coast; "

the rarest of sailing and fishing is afforded along these shores, as
well as camping upon or near them; and every object within sight
from the shifting stand-points, or from rock or tent outlook, suggests
the most interesting reminiscences and historic associations.

But the intrinsic merits of the Plymouth situation, — its air and sunshine, its magnificent and varied scenery, its offered succession of
superlative delights, and withal its recreative qualities, — these consti-
tute its chief attractions for the summer visitor. The town itself, in
its habited portions, is quiet and dreamy enough; realizing, however,
all the conditions of progressive civilization, and appearing among the
Old Colony communities like an ancient barony in the midst of a
venerable district, dignified, well-to-do, intelligent, and not insensible

to the claims of position, or the traditions and experiences of a long and honorable existence. In provision for the needs, the conveniences and enjoyments of her community in every social, business or domestic department, Plymouth is abreast the age and day; and this the sojourning stranger will soon discover, if he will but tarry in her midst long enough to find out that a short mile of village street cannot reveal all her treasures, and that gazing at Pilgrim relics and treading upon hallowed soil are not the only exercises possible in this section which are followed by pleasurable emotions. To tarry awhile in Plymouth is far better than to make a brief pilgrimage to its shrines or monuments.

All along the seashore here, sufficient and often sumptuous hostelries are to be found, while of hospitable private places of entertainment there is no lack. So from the bluffs at Manomet, the sand-dunes of South Plymouth, the plateaus overlooking the great Cove, and the orchards and river bottoms of the Cliff neighborhood, around to the very centre and heart of the town, there is ample accommodation and warm welcome for all well-disposed comers. Not even "Norman's Woe," or the shelving ledges of Pigeon Cove, present so grand standpoints from which to view the rolling surf during a storm at sea, or when the winds are piping high along shore, as does the coast anywhere for a dozen miles southward from the head of the beach in old Plymouth town.

Clustered about the Burial Hill — situated in the very heart of the ancient village — and within view from its summit or sides, are more objects and places of historic interest than many whole States can present. The views seaward are most enchanting; and when the weather is fair and clear, those inland are hardly less pleasing. Perhaps from the very stand-point one occupies on this outlook there springs an antiquated head-stone, setting forth the facts of birth and death of some member of the Mayflower's company. All around in the immediate vicinity are similar relics, in the deciphering of which not altogether unprofitable hours may be spent. Near by, on the hillside, is the site of the old fort, which was also a meeting-house, and where the fathers came up to worship with muskets upon shoulder and swords buckled in place. The hill slopes abruptly at first and then more gently to the water's edge, where lies the remains of the immortal rock under its ornate canopy; and within the interval are Cole's Hill — where Indians and Pilgrims are promiscuously buried, and from which the harbor outlook is of the finest — and the main streets of the town, some of these unchanged in location and principal features since they were laid out by the officers of the Pilgrim company. Off to the right, landward, and looking across the valley or gorge through which runs the stream traced by the Pilgrim Billington to its source, is "Watson's Hill," thick-dotting houses and estates now covering the spots where once the Indian sagamores and braves held their "powwows" and celebrated the feasts incident to their assemblages. In the opposite direction the great monument shows in bold relief, its foundations resting where Massasoit and Samoset once reigned as chieftains, and upon grounds whose historic association is probably only surpassed in interest by that unwritten history enacting since the creation. And on either hand, or in the direction opposite from that in which Old Ocean lies outstretched, the finest landscapes are exposed, stretching away to the horizon.

Looking seaward from the brow of Burial Hill the view is grand indeed. The land-locked harbor, placid as a lake under the summer sun and breezes, is measured by miles in its outlines, and invites irresistibly to water sports of every kind. The roadstead between the harbor and the bay shows in the clear, calm days long-drawn, thread-like lines of whitest surf, which in the distance would appear as though painted on the surface, did they not vanish and change position so constantly. These lines mark the localities where dangers lurk, and where in times past terrible shipwrecks have distinguished the region, of which great mounds upon the hill whereon the gazer stands

PLYMOUTH ROCK AND COLE'S HILL.

further attest. Not far out from the point of the long, slender beach, the "Cow-yard," where the Mayflower lay at anchor while her company landed, is plainly visible in every part of its surface. On the other side and near the Duxbury shore, "Clark's Island," where the Pilgrims passed the first Sabbath, seems to float upon the water and lift its rounded hills and greenest tree-tops in clear contrast to the sun-bleached sands which stretch along for miles beyond and behind. Further inland, on the Duxbury shore, "Captain's Hill," with its unfinished crowning monument to Myles Standish capping the view, rises like a vast pyramid out of a plain, and in a great semicircle beyond the horizon settles down, forming the outlines of the famous bay, on the far side of which in a clear day the tip-end of Cape Cod may be distinctly seen, thus bringing all the prominent localities made famous by the Pilgrims into view from one stand-point.

It was upon the Plymouth shore that John Alden, when he rushed "like an insane man" forth from the presence of the fair Priscilla, after delivering the wooing message of Captain Myles Standish,—

> "Paced up and down the sand, and bared his head to the east wind,
> Cooling his heated brow, and the fire and fever within him.
>
> *   *   *   *   *   *   *   *
>
> ' Welcome, O Wind of the East!' he exclaimed in his wild exultation,
> ' Welcome, O Wind of the East, from the coves of the misty Atlantic!
> Blowing o'er fields of dulse and measureless meadows of sea-grass,
> Blowing o'er rocky wastes, and the grottos and gardens of ocean!
> Lay thy cold, moist hand on my burning forehead, and wrap me
> Close in thy garments of mist, to allay the fever within me!'"

And thousands since his time have paced up and down those sands, or have sat upon the rocks or jutting cliffs overlooking them, and welcomed even as he did the "east wind" with its cooling, grateful influences, allaying alike the fever heats of over-worked humanity, and the fierce summer heats which distinguish the temperate zone. And still, as in the days of old, the sea-breezes blow over "fields of dulse and measureless meadows of sea-grass;" and even while one inhales their breath the salty perfume is mingled with the fragrance of countless wild flowers, which grow in profusion almost to the very surf-line in every part of the coast.

With every year the number of travellers in this section grows larger and larger, and, as discoveries in the directions above outlined are more and more made, the summer population of the locality is vastly increased. Already little colonies, made up sometimes of artists and professional characters, have settled for summering near the inland water sheets above described, or upon the seashore at different points, while individual estates and summer-houses dot the shore and hill-sides in all directions. With all these movements and developments and enlargements the transportation enterprise here alluded to keeps more than even pace, and the finest sections possible for summering purposes are coming rapidly into general knowledge and experience in consequence.

Within half a mile of Burial Hill, and beginning at a point opposite the great Pilgrim monument, the track of the Old Colony Railroad trails along the shore, the windings and turnings of which for upwards of forty miles it is to follow, until Boston is reached. Seven times outward and six times inward each week-day its passenger trains minister to the local wants of the resident population, and to the convenience and satisfaction of thousands of visitors, tourists and pilgrims, who yearly make this town an object of exploration or place of sojourning.

THE BAY AND ITS NEIGHBORHOOD.

BEGINNING at the South Shore and following away round to Provincetown (the "tip-end" of Cape Cod), the broken and indented shore, the coast thus outlined aggregating upwards of 150 miles continuously of tide-mark, the shores here indicated enclose as in a massive basin the entire southern portion of Massachusetts Bay, and form in their general outlines nearly a circle around this water area, the latter being continuously hemmed in on its east, south and west boundaries, and connecting with the waters of which it forms a part only on the north side. This area is from twenty to thirty miles across in nearly all directions, and is sometimes known as "Cape Cod Bay," at least, the portion nearest the Cape lands bear that title. A consultation of the appropriate map forming a part of this book will very nearly explain the situation, only the scale upon which the map must be drawn prevents the representation of all the indentations of the coast line. With the exception of a short "break" in the territory of ancient Plymouth, sections of the Old Colony Railroad follow these bay shores in every part, while both the bay and ocean coasts of Cape Cod (Barnstable County) receive its ministrations, and it sends three distinct and direct lines completely through the Old Colony territory, these connected at various points by spurs and branches, so that the region may truly be described as "gridironed" by this system, and both coast and inland bountifully provided for so far as transportation facilities are concerned.

Now the waters of the bay above referred to have so important a part in all the sanitary, recreative and pleasure-giving features of the section, and enter so largely into the attractions of so great a portion of south-eastern Massachusetts, that any description of the locality which should ignore or leave them out of account, or neglect reference to their peculiar influences upon the region, would be hardly worthy of consideration. The movement occasioned by the tides and the action of the winds and currents of these great surrounding recesses of ocean waters, with the evaporation constantly going forward under the sun's rays and the mingling of a variety of temperatures, have direct and powerful results in all parts of the section upon the quality and tempering of the atmosphere. In her own mysterious ways Nature conducts her operations here as elsewhere, and there is no accounting for her ministrations, which sometimes seem so singularly applied as to be worthy the term of "vagaries." The waters upon the outer shores of Cape Cod are directly within the influence of the great "Gulf Stream," whose heated current passes not many miles away to the

south-eastward, occasionally making its proximity significant in the most remarkable manner. On the shores of Cape Cod Bay, however, the case is different, a distinct thread or stream of the "Arctic Current" being diverted and brought from Labrador to Cape Ann, from whence it runs not far away from the shore lines to the lower part of Cape Cod Bay, following the trend of the land to a section opposite South Plymouth, where it turns abruptly towards the middle of the bay, and, flowing northward in a constantly expanding diffusion, finally loses itself in the ocean waters east of Cape Cod.

The effects of this current, — this clearly marked river in the midst of the waters, — upon the meteorological and sanitary influences of the region is most decided, taken in connection with other conditions, some of which are referred to above. Thus in the town of Plymouth alone, one may often meet with a difference of temperature equal to $10°$, during a ride from the principal village to South Plymouth (seven to ten miles), and what has been regarded as a "hot day" be found suddenly, and by the apparently insignificant passing of a range of hills, to have become delightfully tempered and cooled, as though some magic breath from perpetual shades had been sent especially to relieve. While cruising about on the surface of the bay these effects are if anything still more observable, being often noticed by the unthinking or the ignorant without the slightest reference to their causes, or thought of their true significance. The temperature of this current is about $55°$ the year round; and while the waters from New Bedford to Nantucket are often filled with ice-fields in winter, and sometimes the frozen belt extends almost solidly across the expanse which separates Nantucket from the southern Cape shores, Cape Cod Bay never freezes. So in summer, while the waters in Buzzard's Bay and off the neighboring shores are so warm that one may flounder in them naked during the whole day, with no thought of any sensations but those of pleasure, the Cape Cod Bay waters are so cold as to repel the bather who does not seek the secluded beaches; and this low temperature influences and modifies not alone the atmosphere of all the surrounding shores, as well as that of the bay itself, but it proves a potent factor in averting the attacks of thunder-storms, which, especially about Plymouth and the South Shore, have fairly to fight their way against it, and are usually sent off in roundabout courses to other sections.

But the chief attractions of the waters of this bay for the summer sojourner, as well as for the dweller on its shores, are of a far different order than those thus indicated. It is not the land, but the water, which one seeks upon visiting the seashore, or, rather the union of land and water scenes, advantages and enjoyments. The bathing, the boating, the fishing, the exciting races in the swift yacht when the billows dance merrily and the breezes blow lustily; the tussle with the gamey bluefish, while the fleet craft fairly flies before the half gale prevailing; the morning twilight excursion to lovely ledges and mysterious feeding-grounds far off the shore, where cod and haddock and hake, and peradventure the ignoble dog-fish, reward the efforts; the "trying" for mackerel, or the drailing in the tideways or currents for the striped bass. And if one is sojourning on the lower Cape shores, and makes acquaintance with some adventurous skippers of that region, what more likely than that he may witness, become identified with in fact, a genuine whale hunt, a chase after Leviathan in the most primitive style, with no whit of the ancient excitement, dangers or interests of such occupation abated, and all its attributes a thousand fold enhanced through the novelty and exhilaration of the occasion. That this noble sport has not entirely disappeared from Massachusetts waters, along with the decadence of Nantucket and New Bedford as whaling ports, what follows here may explain, although popular ideas may not have run in line with the narration for many a day. The following account of a day's whaling in the bay will better illustrate one feature of its possibilities than countless words of general description : —

The denizens of Cape Cod have always been an amphibious population, largely taking their living from, and making their fortunes upon, the waters of the ocean of the world. Especially is this the case with the people of the lower half of the "right arm," who are fishers indeed, the majority of them taking to the water, like young ducks, immediately after their advent into a sandy world, and becoming experts in the navigation of its depths and the captors of its treasures even before their school-days have fully passed.

Provincetown occupies the extremity — the curling finger — of this cape, and its situation is in every way peculiar. With the exception of a narrow strip or neck of sand-heaps which unites it to the main cape, it is surrounded by water — the salt water of the Atlantic — which rolls unchecked between its shores and those of Europe. Its coast line, beginning at a point opposite the narrow neck alluded to, sweeps around in a grand circle almost the entire circuit of the compass, its outlines nearly resembling those of a gigantic capital C. The inclosed water of this circle is the harbor of Provincetown, and the town is built along the inner shore, at the bottom of the basin. Outside is the Race, Wood End, and sundry interesting points of lighthouse, life-saving station, etc., all of vast moment to mariners and ship-owners. Inside is one of the singular harbors of the world, deep enough and spacious enough to shelter a fleet of hundreds of the largest ships at one time; and with peculiarities belonging to itself sufficient to make it famous wherever these ships may sail.

If there are any kinds of fish, or any methods of taking them, which are not familiar to the people of Provincetown, their description is now in order. From the fry and minnow for pickerel bait up to the 100-barrel right whale, Provincetown waters have witnessed the capture of all kinds, and have frequently contributed specimens over which savants have puzzled and wondered. The beaches of her shores have received as loot mighty carcases of whales and blackfish; shoals of porgies at one time which all the teams of the region could hardly remove soon enough, so immense was the deposit; while fish-weirs, try-works, and the implements and appliances of various fisheries mark the scene in all directions.

Now, it has been no unusual thing, at any time since the establishment of this exaggerated fish-net yclept Provincetown, for a whale of some variety to be occasionally stranded upon her beaches, or captured by her cruisers or boatmen. A whale in the harbor of Provincetown, especially at certain seasons, is almost as common a presence as that of a turtle in a mill-pond; but they are usually representatives of a class disliked and scorned by old-school whalemen, and not remunerative to their capturers, unless the latter be men of enthusiasm and desperate enterprise.

The variety of whale mostly found in Massachusetts Bay waters is the finback, a long, clean, perfectly formed creature, growing sometimes to seventy-five or eighty feet in length, but usually from forty-

· BLACKFISH ·

five to fifty-five feet. He is the most complete model of craft for speed and easy working in the water that can be imagined, and his tail in motion the most perfect development of the screw motor; and, indeed, the finback moves through the water when occasion offers as the most rapid express train does on its tracks on land. It is timid and non-resistant, and it is principally on account of its great speed and its habit of immediate flight when stricken that the whalemen detest it. Your veteran has no relish for being drawn to the bottom, boat and all, by an aquatic race-horse possessing the travelling qualities of a meteor.

Therefore, the youngsters, who are perpetually learning new "kinks" and confounding their progenitors, have stepped into another order of things. They begin with an exact reversal of the old-time processes, which were to harpoon the whale, and then lance him to death. The Provincetowner first lances his prey, and immediately after harpoons it, for reasons and in pursuance of methods shortly to be given.

The finbacks come in numbers early in the spring, following the bait which is their food — herrings, sand eels, mackerel, and the like, and where this bait is found in reasonable quantities the whale will surely appear. When feeding, this whale stretches wide open his jaws, moves forward among the bait on the surface with velocity until he has pocketed or scooped (in his mouth) a quantity (some barrels), when he snaps together his front doors and swallows the catch, having no teeth, nor need of any. It is at this feeding season that he is easiest approached and fastened to. When not feeding he is naturally lazily sleeping, or disporting; and, indeed, the gambols of this variety of whale seem to form a very necessary part of his existence, to which he pays much attention. The antics of a calf in a pasture, or a young puppy in a back yard, are hardly more diverting or singular than are those of a pair of whales in their festive moments. They will stand on their heads and flourish their tails in the air, then stand upon their tails and snap their jaws in the air. They whirl and roll and swash about, sometimes tearing the water into shreds, and exhausting every possibility of whale enjoyment. They are as full of curiosity as a deer, and this they evidence frequently by playing about the boats which have come out to capture them, reconnoitering and viewing these from all sides, and, sinking a few feet below the surface, following their every motion, while they occasionally appear at the surface for an outside observation.

When touched or struck their immediate impulse is to dash off like a rocket, and this impulse they obey to perfection. To test their marvellous facility of speed, a harpoon was thrown into one off the Race (the extremity of Cape Cod), when he started across the bay in the direction of Boston, and in forty minutes had dragged the boat and its contents of crew and implements within full view of Minot's Ledge lighthouse. All the line was played out by the boat's crew, and they were finally obliged to slip for their lives.

The bomb lance is a most destructive weapon. The gun from which the lance is fired is of very thick metal, and the breech is made heavy with lead, to neutralize the recoil, which is excessive with this kind of arm. The length of barrel is about seventeen inches. The lance itself is of iron, with a chamber six or seven inches in length along the lower centre, and solid between the chamber and point, the latter tapering, and filed or ground to three edges. About the base of the lance are India rubber wings, folded when the lance is inserted in the gun, and acting as wad to make the lance fit the barrel easily, and just rest upon the powder charge of the gun. When fired, these rubber wings expand, and, like the paper feathers of a boy's dart, preserve the poise of the weapon. The chamber of the lance is filled with powder, like a bomb-shell, and a one-second, or thereabout, fuse is attached, so that, when the weapon is discharged into the body of a whale, it explodes within, inflicting terrible wounds. Care must be taken not to discharge the lance at too short range, as in that case it will pass through and through the whale's carcase without exploding, and entail no serious injury. About thirty feet distance is the range usually sought for. This implement, in the hands of a cool and skilful sailor, works "like a charm," and great is its destruction of the life of Leviathan. To illustrate the whole matter, an actual day's work will now be detailed.

At two o'clock on a morning in May of a recent season, the crew of a whaling schooner was aroused by the captain, the vessel then lying near the wharves in Provincetown harbor. She was got under way, and the spouting or "blowing" of a whale could be plainly heard from her deck. At once the chase began, the experienced captain working in the dark, at times with prospects of success, but without its attainment as the hours passed. That there was more than one whale in the harbor was evident, and one of them a humpback, a prize, indeed, and much more valuable than a finback, yielding twice as much of oil for the same size of creature. As dawn streaked and day opened, one after another various other craft in the harbor became awakened to what was going on, and numerous boats' crews put off from the shore to join in a chase and possible capture, with the details of which they were perfectly familiar, and the tactics of which were their common practice.

The first rays of the sun fell upon an exciting scene. There was a humpback whale and a finback coursing about the harbor, the latter fully sixty-five feet in length. The chasing boats and vessels represented a great variety of craft, and a still greater variety of crews and individuals engaged. There were tall, short, crooked, lank, old and young boatsteerers; fat men puffing at paddles, and lean men tugging at long oars. Excitement, emulation and competition roused all these men to prodigious efforts, and, in their anxiety and enthusiasm, they manifested the most singular traits and cut the oddest pranks. The finback led them a desperate chase, now here, now there, until hours had slipped away, and he was not caught, although the very elite of Cape Cod skill in whale capture, aided by experienced veterans of the northern and Pacific fleets, had lent a hand. Away over on the east side of the harbor the humpback was finally stricken, a bomb lance entering his huge body, shattering his backbone in the explosion, and the monster died instantly. A vigorous and triumphant yell announced the capture, but the finback escaped. The schooner then proceeded outside, and followed the shore towards the Race.

From the time of leaving the harbor until noon not a whale was sighted. About noon it fell flat calm, and the schooner drifted lazily. But as the early afternoon advanced, the cry of "Blows!" awoke every man to the knowledge that an immediate change in status might be at hand. The sun was burning hot, and the face of the bay like a mirror. In less time after the first cry than it takes to tell the incident, no less than fifteen "blows" were counted, and whales were in abundance on every hand.

The boat, which had been towing astern, was at once occupied, and the advance was made without delay. The spouting columns appeared at regular intervals, and soon the chase was in close proximity. Headway was stopped, the oarsmen exchanged their oars for stumpy paddles, like those with which an Indian manages his canoe, and every one of them took his seat upon the gunwale of the boat, paddles in hand, ready for orders. The captain took his stand forward, gun at poise, ready to discharge the lance at the first favorable opportunity. The whales (there were two of them, male and female, as it proved) were sportive, and at once began a reconnoisance of the boat. Their every motion could be plainly seen while they were under water, and their movements anticipated. The captain singled out the female, the largest and best animal, and thenceforth all attention was paid to her movements. At last she came slowly to the surface, just moved her immense tail with the necessary motion to change her direction, and started directly across the bow of the boat, under the very nose of the captain. A straightforward shot was what he had been waiting for, and in an instant the gun was at his shoulder. As the gigantic finback passed — she proved to be upwards of sixty-five feet in length — she rolled slightly to one side, and threw up the flipper nearest the captain, as a man would throw up the elbow of his bent arm to a level with the shoulder. Quick as thought the captain fired, the lance struck the huge carcase just under the flipper and entirely disappeared, and the empty gun was flung along the bottom of the boat. Instantly the captain was standing on the bow deck, harpoon in hand. The whale was motionless, apparently with absolute astonishment. In this moment of quiet, which could not be prolonged, the boat slightly advanced, the captain's both hands rose high in the air, the harpoon descended directly downward, and the whale was transfixed, the iron entering her body near the tail. The lance had seemingly hardly left the gun at greater speed than the initial movement of that whale when consciousness was aroused. The whale line attached to the harpoon was coiled with characteristic care in two tubs nearly amidships, led aft around the loggerhead in the stern deck, and then forward through a notch in the extreme bow, out of which it was kept from slipping by a pin passed through the two upper parts of the crotch. Instantly every man was standing along this line, grasping it with hat in hand to preserve it from the intense friction. The loggerhead was kept constantly wet, and a man stood over it, hatchet in hand, to cut upon the first "foul," or other indication of extreme danger. And now appeared the wisdom of the movements. The lance had entered the vitals of the whale, inflicting, it was well known, a terrible internal wound upon its explosion. Had this not been the case, and only the harpoon held the whale, she would have finished the race incontinently by obliging the crew to slip the line, or be drawn under water. As it was, she must soon come up for further action. The whale moved forward and also downward, and the water was there many fathoms deep. The downward

movement of course depressed the bow of the boat, and the immediate
danger was from being drawn under by motion too swift to allow
the cutting of the surface. At once a great trough was made in the
smooth sea by the flying craft, the boat occupying the cavity, and from
both her sides a sloping bank of water, inclining outward and upward,
seemed builded about her. To one sitting upon a thwart and looking
outward, the surface of the bay seemed just opposite the line of the
eyes, so great was the depression of the trough.

Now, then, a sheer of the whale and the boat would take water at
once over the side. The forward movement became too swift, the bow
too much depressed. Fathom after fathom was allowed to slip around
the loggerhead, until 50, 60, 80, 100 fathoms had been paid out, and
three or four minutes had elapsed. The whale had been struck off the
Race, and had started across the bay in the direction of Plymouth.

YACHTING IN THE BAY.

At the end of the time indicated the line began to slack and the whale
to move upward from the bottom of the bay. Still, however, she tore
onward. As fast as could be the line was hauled upon, and all possible
taken in. And now the whale is upon the surface, and great jets of
almost pure blood, red and arterial, rise in the air and fall backward
upon her head and shoulders. That tells the story! The boat rushes
forward, and seems to be floating in blood, so thick have the waters
become with it, and the smell arising is deadly sickening and almost
suffocating to the inexperienced.

Down again the creature goes, to remain about the same time as at
first. The speed hardly diminishes. Up again she comes, and now
the noise of her spouting is as of huge pipes obstructed, and soon great

clots of blood and substance fall upon the surface as before. Every muscle in every man is as tense as whalebone, and every nerve like steel. Each says to himself, "Will the end never be?"

A breeze is rising on the eastern board, but its outer edge is still far from the schooner. The two men left on board the latter have headed her in chase of the boat, but she is soon hull down in the view of the boat's crew. No matter! Suddenly the whale turns square about, and starts back toward the Race. There is some confusion, a slacking and jerking of the line, and all at once the harpoon slips, and whale and boat are parted. And now the men growl and lower at the captain, for letting their hard-earned prize thus escape. But he knows that a short time must decide the contest, and that the whale must soon die.

She is followed by her frequent spoutings of black blood and matter, and, her speed slackening, the chase draws upon her. She stops. Will the captain give her another lance?

And now she leaps full length out of the water, and falls prone upon it with a crash like a falling building. The surface is streaked and torn with foam mingled with blood. She stands now upon her head, now upon her tail; like lightning she darts hither and thither. She sinks and rises, spouts and half rolls over. Every man is in position to keep clear of her, if in her frenzy she blindly comes their way. "For God's sake, captain, look out!" shouts one; "here she comes!" The warning is justified; she is coming full head toward the boat. But momently she staggers, ceases effort; her motion slows; she rolls three-quarters over, and lies dead in the middle of Cape Cod Bay.

Even so the waters of this bay yield constantly the greatest variety of wonderful attractions for the sojourner along their shores, and unfold new beauties and enticements with every passing hour. What glorious sailing courses are afforded by its conformation, between points miles apart and over distances fairly studded with the associations which have accumulated through centuries! The canoes of the Indian passed hundreds of years ago over the very section where, afterwards, the exploring shallops of the Pilgrims became familiar, and the strange sounding names which to the present day distinguish the points and headlands and various localities hereabouts, were bestowed long before the region became civilized under the austere influences of the Pilgrim Fathers and their successors. Saquish, Manomet, Patuxet, Indian Hill, — a hundred appellations bestowed when the region knew no other than a savage tenantry, and all these having most appropriate significance, lend a peculiar charm to the sections they designate.

Within the limits of every town having shores upon the bay, there are sure to be found bathing facilities of the first order. Strips of white sand beach, enclosed or sheltered nooks along the shore line, where the warm sun-rays, falling upon the sands while the tide is out, heat them thoroughly in every part, and when the waters come in at the turn of the tide they are deliciously tempered as they make slowly

over the gleaming waste, and receive the bather as though they had
been prepared especially for his delectation, as indeed they have. Parties from far inland find no more satisfactory feature in seashore life
than that afforded by ocean bathing; and nowhere are sea-baths more
perfectly afforded, or their furnishings more completely and lavishly
provided, than along the shores of this bay and the south coasts of
Massachusetts, including the marvellous islands (Nantucket, Martha's
Vineyard, etc.,) which sentinel those parts.

As for the pedestrian excursions along the shores of the bay, the walks
at morning or evening or mid-day, with the most enchanting bits of land
scenery springing inland from all points on the one hand, and Old
Ocean rolling his waters at one's very feet on the other; the variety
and the quantities of the shells which are crumbled beneath the tread
at every step forward; the curious geological specimens of minute
formation which the pebble patches reveal; the singular beauty and
profusion of the myriad manifestations of marine grasses and weeds,
—long ribbons, apparent fruit clusters, or matted thickets of vegeta-
tion which cling to the rocks as though their roots pierced to the centres, and these animate with marine fishes or animalculæ most inviting
to note or study; the great rock-masses, bare and iron brown at low
tide, and surf-beaten and grandly invincible when the waters are up
and the elements are striving. There is hardly a mile of all these
coasts that has not witnessed a shipwreck; and some of these points,
where the walks are superlatively attractive and the entertainment
most lavishly bestowed, have noted scores of terrible marine tragedies
during their association with human existence, and have been thickly
strewn with bodies which have made sad landing upon them, from
ill-fated crafts, whose bones, even now, are distributed in the clefts
of the rocks, or lie half-buried in the sands, rotting under the sky.

CAPE COD.

QUAINT Cape Cod! Even its name has a flavor of oddity about it which illustrates the grim humor of the Pilgrim delegation selecting it. Fishing in its neighboring waters, the party decided that the first fish caught should give title to the new-found cape; and up from the bottom speedily whisked a goodly cod—and "Cape Cod" was immediately christened into existence.

For pure and unadulterated seashore delights, the "Right Arm" of the Old Bay State has no superior anywhere. Scarcely more than five miles in width in any part, it extends outward from the main-land for upwards of sixty miles, its inner shores washed by the waters of one of the most picturesque bays known to the world, while its outer coast-line presents a barrier to the broad Atlantic, which rolls in magnificent surf-beats from end to end of its territory, illustrating every mood of Old Ocean, from the placid quiet of the summer calms to the angry fury of hurricane-swept waters, rushing overwhelmingly upon the land. Every variety of ocean scenery and attraction is presented by this section: the irregular surf-line, extending often for miles on either hand, broken by headlands and inlets and winding beaches; the deadly "bars" off the land, over which the waters madly dash and break and roar when the storms are on, and showing long lines of silver threads and patches of lace-work when ocean forces are in mildest slumber; the great cliffs of white-gleaming sands, crowned with beneficent light-towers and frowning over far-stretching beaches, from any part of which glorious outlooks upon the ocean expanse may be had. Here are always cool and quiet retreats upon the land, while the waters offer the fairest opportunities for boating, fishing, bathing, and infinite study and experience, which can be found where land and water meet. The waters of the bay afford the most exciting pursuit of the whale, blackfish or porpoise, if one is bent upon heroic sport, or for the bass and gamey bluefish for more tempered excitement. And on all sides the Cape one may indulge the passion or the predeliction for sailing, utilizing every condition for the purpose, from the zephyr blowing over a surface of mill-pond smoothness, to a half-gale and ocean waves rolling majestically.

The popular idea of Cape Cod, as held by those who have never visited that section, is largely misleading; nor is it certain that even those persons who have made occasional "flying" trips to its localities have thoroughly appreciated the place. A series of dunes and bluffs covering miles in extent; heavy, sand-laden roads over which vehicles toil with the utmost difficulty; treeless, almost verdureless barren plains, wind-swept and bleak; a population coarse and cross-grained, and quaint with the eccentricities of ignorance and isolated condition — these, and

+MAP OF+

ld Colony Railroad,

CAPE COD DIVISION.

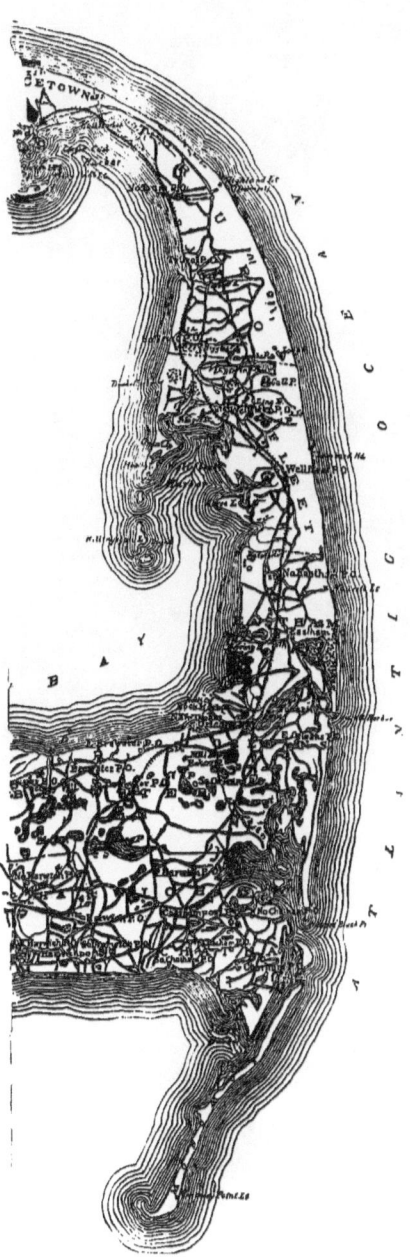

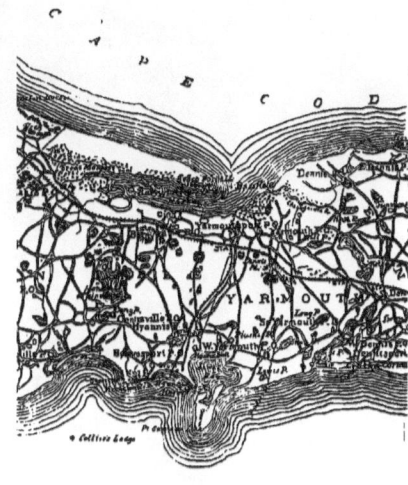

of
or
ng
ed
n
"

such as these, are the attributes popularly credited to the region, and form the estimates too often entertained by intelligent people, who would need but the merest peep at the actual situation to become disabused of the false notions. Cape Cod, although sandy enough naturally, and often presenting that feature with a prominence that cannot be disregarded, is nevertheless not in the least a desert waste; on the contrary, it presents some of the finest fancy farms and grass lands in the Commonwealth, and its roads and driveways are far better made and more comfortable to travel over, than can often be found inland in Massachusetts. For fine old trees, shading thoroughly hand-some village streets, not many towns in New England can surpass Yarmouth and other upper sections; while the specialty farms of the Barnstable villages and the grass lands of Eastham — representing nearly the two extremes of the Cape, emphatically give the lie to stories of barrenness and unproductive conditions. The alternating patches of cranberry grounds, thickly strewn through the Barnstable, Yarmouth, Dennis, Harwich and other townships, and which appear the "Dutch kitchens" of agriculture, so fair and smooth and neat are they, are marvellously pretty gardens in summer time, and with the alternating groves and meadow plats suf-ficiently break the monotony of scenery such as must inevitably exist upon a land-strip sur-rounded by ocean waters. As to the people — mistakes regarding them are more easily made than in the cases already referred to. Cape Cod sea captains and offi-cers are to be found in every port of the earth, as well as in all its nooks and corners, and this has been true for two centuries, or such a matter; and as these

WIND-MILL ON THE CAPE.

sharp representatives of the keenest Yankee race have always delighted to take their wives and daughters about the world with them, and the sons have made the same "cruises" on their own account, it hap-pens that in every dozen of Cape Cod families there are more indi-viduals who have "seen the world," than can be found in any one hundred families elsewhere on earth. These matters are alluded to that the reader may be assured of the fact that it is possible to fall far short of a correct estimate of this tongue of land, in any respect.

It is hardly necessary, however, to assure anybody who knows aught of its real situation of the superior claims of Cape Cod as a summering-place, for it can be nothing short of the best in this regard, so far as sea-coast sojourning is concerned. It makes little difference in what part of the Cape the summer visitor may decide to tarry, or whether he concludes to visit many portions in turn; he will find peculiar attractions in all. For purely ocean scenes and influences, Provincetown, Truro, Wellfleet, and the middle towns will present special features. Immense hotels, crowded with guests and brilliant with all the fashionable paraphernalia, form no part of any existing attributes of Cape Cod summering. But there are quiet private houses, where hospitality, good cheer, and a home-life unequalled for its grateful ministrations may be secured, within reach of recreative enjoyments which can never be understood or appreciated except as matters of experience. The ocean in storm and calm; the life-saving stations, grouped more thickly on these shores than anywhere else; the peculiar employments, facilities and pursuits of the population; the beautiful shore scenery; the light establishment; the fisheries; the singular make-up and grouping of the habitations and villages; the ancient Yankee manners and customs; all these, with the matters enumerated above and many others not here presented, render this section a paradise of summer enjoyments.

On the upper section, from Hyannis around to Wood's Holl, whereof some idea may be obtained by consulting the accompanying map, many of the best ocean features and attributes are presented, while those of more inland localities are added. The scenery and outlooks characterizing this portion of the Cape are indeed magnificent; and whether one walks or drives along the shore neighborhoods, or whiles away the hours in boating off and on, the results of perfect contentment and delight are sure to follow. The bluffs along these shores are dotted with little hamlets formed by summer residences, which appear perfect bowers of elegance and comfort, of which the Cotochesset House and its neighborhood, and scores other of similar situations, are typical. Hither to such places come every summer representatives of the best conditions of life in every part of our country, and the traveller from foreign parts is sure to be delighted by the charms here spread out on every hand. Few people have any correct idea of the rapidity of the growth of this section. From Wood's Holl, the Falmouth, Cotuit and succeeding shores away round to Hyannis, are undergoing most complete transformations, and now rival the Connecticut and Long Island coasts in the beauty and lavish provision of their establishments; while for natural attractiveness, fine scenery and as sanitary resorts, they have no superiors, if they have equals, anywhere. These statements are easily verified — a single trip through the region will settle the matter; and it would be folly indeed to thus represent the case if it could be readily overthrown, or brought to contempt and dishonor.

Upon Cape Cod (as well as Nantucket) are to be found preserved the ancient types and customs of New England. Here are the original flavor and atmosphere which distinguished the region in the old colonial days, and grew out of the conditions of life imposed by the "Forefathers." Some of the Cape Cod settlements are of little later date than that of Plymouth; indeed, it is usual, even so near the locality as Boston city, to consider the ancient town of Plymouth as belonging to and a part of Cape Cod, which, however, it is not, only Barnstable

HIGHLAND LIGHT

PUBLIC LIBRARY ORLEANS

WATER MILL AT Cotuit

PICKING CRANBERRIES

The OCEAN from CHATHAM

VIEWS ON CAPE COD

PROVINCETOWN HARBOR

County being included in that charmed section. Very many people suppose, and base statements upon the supposition, that the Cape includes all the shore section south from Cohasset, and the South Shore towns are also frequently spoken of as "Cape Cod" localities.

As has been well said, "the whole Massachusetts coast is Art ground," —but preëminently the shores of southern Cape Cod, and from these points away round to New Bedford and Newport, must be reckoned in that connection. Every foot of this territory and its noble outlooks is known to artists of name in their profession, and both landscape and marine studies are afforded here in richest profusion. On the upper Cape—in and about the Sandwich, Falmouth and Barnstable woods, there are successions of the most beautiful drives, with constant surprises awaiting one,—bits of ocean scenery coming unexpectedly into view; mirror-faced ponds or lakelets appearing like marvels of conjuring, and forming parts of landscapes which enchant the novice. Strange though it may appear, considering the formation of the Cape territory, a chain of these ponds or miniature lakes extends far down the centre of this narrow land-tongue, many of them stocked naturally with fine fish, and some of them large enough to present boating facilities vieing with those of the surrounding ocean in excellence and desirableness. The prevailing forest growth for all the Cape below Sandwich and Falmouth is the dwarf pitch pine, the "needles" of which, full of highly-spiced perfume and resinous juices, undoubtedly add much to the health-giving, recreative qualities of the section, as they appear to be surcharged with the principle of vitality, and in their evergreen capacities diffuse invigorating influences the whole year through. In Sandwich, Falmouth and Barnstable the Quaker element is found largely in admixture with the population, with all that is thereby implied of thrift, orderly life, and those attributes of progressive well-to-do humanity which mean so much wherever they are found. The peculiar rural community such as is described in the novel, "Cape Cod Folks," is met with here and there throughout the Cape districts, the particular hamlet and its denizens made famous in the work just referred to being a part of Plymouth, or just about upon the dividing line between Plymouth and Sandwich. Mashpee is the last remaining home of the Indian representatives on the main-land of southern Massachusetts; and the specimens here to be found present more of the social and domestic features of the whites than of the original tribal divisions from which they are descended. In their pursuits they are fishermen; and some of them have developed considerable aptitude in intellectual and business directions.

A list of the names of prominent or famous persons from every walk in life, who with their families every summer make pilgrimage to Cape Cod, might surprise persons who suppose that the representatives of wealth and culture and the highest orders of "society" are only to be found congregated in the great "fashionable" centres, or herding, as it were, in the caravansaries of world-wide renown. From the headquarters of the United States Fish Commission at Wood's Holl, where Prof. Baird and his staff occupy the whole season through, away down the Cape to the "jumping-off place," are the resorts or the summer houses which distinguished men and women occupy; and one soon finds, who comes here for sojourn, that there is no lack of companionable elements, wherever he may have pitched his tent. The Falmouth neighborhood contains whole summer communities of this order. Barnstable, with its villages and outlying districts on both the outer and inner shores of the Cape, shows these features significantly. Sandwich, Yarmouth, Dennis, Brewster, Harwich, Chatham, Orleans, Eastham, Wellfleet, Truro, Provincetown — not one of these towns or their villages but have attracted since the earliest times distinguished visitors to themselves during summer days, who can hardly be made to believe that any other spot than some portion of Cape Cod is fit to breathe upon in summer, at least during a large portion of the time. It may here be said that all the Cape towns, excepting Falmouth, Mashpee, Harwich, Brewster and Chatham, stretch across the Cape, and have both ocean and bay shores.

The advantages growing out of this state of things, both as regards sanitary and pleasure-giving conditions, may readily be estimated.

A peculiar advantage offered by this section is the unequalled facilities it presents for the summering of children. Here is afforded the widest range among the largest combination of health-giving influences, and here the little folks are safe, secluded, and sure to be happy. Of youthful sports and pastimes of the varieties most appreciated and naturally sought after by them, there is no stint; and here they are easily cared for and kept "within ken" continually. There is nothing belittling or demoralizing in early association and familiarity with Old Ocean and his surroundings; and the institutions peculiar to the borders of his realm, the life and light-stations and shore establishments of every kind, imitations in their way of the beneficence and providence of humanity's Creator, have nothing in their moulding or educational influences in common with the doubtful haunts of the great centres or the levelling institutions of conventional localities. Here they may enjoy air-baths, sun-baths or water-baths, singly or all combined; and enlarge their miniature frames and lay foundations of stamina and constitutional elements which all the influences of city or far inland life cannot thereafter throughout the year entirely overthrow. It is the form of life they love, too; for childhood takes as naturally to the water and water scenes as does old age to the chimney corners and grateful retirement.

There are some fascinating haunts along the lower, or southern, Cape Cod coasts, some nooks and corners "stowed away," as her sailors would say, along these shores, that one might well feel proud to fittingly describe; because some of the first artists of the world, in pen or pencil portraiture, who have become enamored of them, have found adequate interpretation of the same most difficult, so far as the appreciation of people who have never seen the places alluded to is concerned. This section of shore is marked by rapidly succeeding indentations, where the salt floods "make inward" upon the land, having scooped or hollowed out for themselves in the process of centuries basins large or small, or deeply embayed cuts, with gently sloping banks on either side, or bolder hill-sides coming down to meet the shores, and these often crowned or bordered with fairest woods growth. The shores of

SUMMER COTTAGE ON CAPE COD.

these estuaries are often fine, smooth beaches, or sedge-grown marshes alternating, and in their immediate vicinity on the land the grandest building-sites imaginable are to be found. Many of these, in the neighborhood of such places as Cotuit, and various Falmouth localities, as well as along the Barnstable shores, have been utilized for summer hotels, or for private dwellings, which present in their most complete aspects the abodes of New England hospitality and entertainment. The ocean expanses lying between these shores and the outer islands (Nantucket and Martha's Vineyard) form the great highway for shipping passing to and from Boston and ports south of her latitude. Of fishing and fowling, in their season, there is no end. On every hand the scenes are the fairest and in their æsthetic qualities the most influential, and here are perfect rest, content, and all that can minister to mind and body diseased, or give these perfect enjoyment in health. Here are to be found some of the most notable hosts and hostelries on the Atlantic coasts, and the associations are with many generations succeeding of manly men, and with events, local or enlarged in their

significance, which lend peculiar interest to their reminiscences and the
legends and traditions growing out of them. Judge and jury, advocate
and client, poet and painter, statesman and politician, merchant and
customer, parson and layman, madam and maid, titled foreigner and
backwoodsmen from the heart of the continent — all comers here are
equally gratified and satisfied with their experiences; and the tide of
summer visitation includes within its volume even greater varieties
of humanity than are above outlined. This is the growing, the significant section of Cape Cod shores, with reference to future importance
as a watering-place. Some of the finest summer cottages to be found
on any coast have been completed or are contracted for in this neighborhood.

The backbone of Cape Cod, and the beneficent minister to every part
of the section as above set forth, is the Old Colony Railroad. Its summer business in this region has grown until the most lavish provision
of train service and accommodations has become its assured practice.
Its trips of trains and connecting boats are made by daylight, and
always with special reference to the fact that its patrons are of " the
cream " of the land, and that service in accordance is in order. In
fact, the same qualities which make of the Fall River and Newport and
Sound lines the finest service offered to the travelling public, are
extended to every part of the system; and as it has no obscure or
unimportant sections within its visitation, there is no discrimination in
the distribution of these qualities.

MARTHA'S VINEYARD.

HE island of "Martha's Vineyard," lying like Nantucket off the shores of south-eastern Massachusetts and much nearer to them, received its name even earlier than did the ancient town which shelters Plymouth Rock, Capt. Gosnold having christened the place in 1602. The origin or significance of the name is unknown, although popular legends have from time to time been invented or "discovered" to fit it; but there is no mistaking the fact that whether used in a sentimental or descriptive sense, a perfect natural garden or vineyard the locality certainly is, and worthy to be named for any of the fairest Marthas or Marys of the earth. Lying considerably less than a half-score miles from the main-land, and divided from the latter by a "reach" of ocean which forms a natural highway for shipping of every kind, as well as a watery expanse charming through its associations with the most beautiful shores, this celebrated island long since became a princely

summering-place, and its fame extended to the uttermost parts of the country. Its connection, too, with one of the most important religious establishments of the land, which since 1835 has utilized its glorious situations for summer camp-meeting purposes, at which the magnates of a prominent denomination from every section have annually congregated, and worshippers by thousands have assembled during the summer months, adds interest to the situation. Without doubt, had not this been the case, the island would have become celebrated as a watering-place, its fine location, excellent sanitary conditions, beautiful features and most favored ocean surroundings, rendering it impossible that the place should have been overlooked in the search for the most perfect summer haunts.

"The Vineyard," as this island is familiarly called, does not differ much in general conformation or physical features from its neighbor, Nantucket; but it has more territory, and being nearer the main-land has not that isolated quality which characterizes the last-named locality. The island is upwards of twenty-five miles in length from north to south, and has several townships within its borders. Some of the most famous roadsteads — as Holmes' Hole, Vineyard Sound, etc., — are among its surrounding waters, and its neighboring small islands are fair spots of earth, displaying the finest verdure and

there
or des
certaii
Marys
from 1
which
a wat
beauti
summ
extenc
of the
too, v
portar
of thc
has ut
tions
purpo:
of a
from
ly con
the su
had n
brated
dition:
render
the sea
"Tl
much
Nantu
has n
localit
north
of the
etc.,—
island

foliage in the summer months, and inviting always to the delights of camping and exploration.

Whatever of excellences of climate or sanitary conditions any of the localities of this region can boast are enjoyed to the fullest degree on Martha's Vineyard. Owing to the peculiar conformation and the extent of this island, it has many natural landing-places for shipping, and as a haven for yacht, or in fact any kind of sailing, fleets it has no superior in the northern Atlantic waters. Its ocean outlooks in every part are of the finest; and for what may be styled purely marine pleasures, boating, sailing, and the occupations which arise out of a constant visitation on every side of numberless sea-craft, it has no equal on our coasts. Holmes' Hole is a natural harbor of refuge, and here, during head winds or "stress of weather," hundreds of vessels are sometimes found for days together, awaiting more favorable circumstances, their crews meanwhile helping to make matters lively on shore, and materially adding to the numbers of the transient population.

And as the waters round about Martha's Vineyard present the finest and most acceptable highways for yachting and boating, so the gently rolling grounds of the island and its long reaches of level country offer the most excellent drives, the adjuncts of which are peculiar to the place, which almost in every part is in full view of the ocean. Every breeze which prevails here must of necessity be tempered by ocean influences, and the summer winds are deliciously cool and invigorating, even while only a few miles inland on the main the most enervating heats are prevailing. The sail from the wharf at Wood's Holl to the landing at the Bluffs is over only seven miles of distance; and various points of land lie about on every hand, offering fairest rewards and enjoyments for excursionists and variety for the enterprising and vigorous summer sojourner.

Oak Bluffs—the "Cottage City," one of the "institutions" of this country,—was the direct outgrowth of the camp-meeting planting, and is now about two-score of years old. The fame of the Martha's Vineyard camp-meetings has gone out through all the earth, and none now need to be told that this form of religious worship long since attained its greatest proportions here. From the first foundation of these meetings there were those among their regular attendants who found in the place not only sacred and valued associations growing out of its connection with the religious establishment, but a situation fair to view and desirable to occupy; and these became habituated to anticipating the meeting season in their attendance, and remaining behind after the religious exercises were finished—in fact, they became summer residents, building cottages or temporary homes, and in every way providing for making their stay comfortable and pleasant. In course of time other and richer visitors, attracted sometimes by the novelty of the meeting establishment, and still more, perhaps, by the superlative charms of the island, added their presence and their villas and ornate cottages to the general assemblage, until the renowned "Cottage City"

BATH TOWER
AND
BATHERS.
Cottage City

GAY HEAD

SEA VIEW HOUSE
Cottage City

SAMOSET AVE
COTTAGE CITY

MARTHA'S
VINEYARD

had taken place, a community point which is now one of the wonders of the western world, and which has not its counterpart anywhere else. Great and small hotels, restaurants, libraries, all sorts of public conveniences and appliances, are in fullest provision; and here one may find largest scope for all his ideas, or practices growing out of them, with regard to summering; making one with the great throng in a notable caravansary; mingling with the most cultured guests or temporary denizens of the ideal summer houses of the place; becoming a dweller in tents or rude lodgings, like the patriarchs of old; or he may sojourn by himself in some chosen nook or solitude, philosophizing or exploring or investigating alone, like Thoreau, up and down the shores, or like the heroes or the old red sand-stone.

The shores of Martha's Vineyard are of surpassing attractiveness, and their fascinations are greatly enhanced through the animation which always prevails upon the surrounding waters. All the marine

GAY HEAD, MARTHA'S VINEYARD.

travel between New York and the North and Boston and the South passes through Holmes' Hole and Vineyard Sound, and these bits of ocean are always alive with shipping. The shores of the island are overhung in many parts with bluffs or cliffs, and occasionally the fairest islets lie separated from the "mother island" by only a narrow strip of ocean water. The "Sea View Boulevard" follows the south shore from Oak Bluffs to Katama, a distance of ten miles, making one of the most beautiful driveways imaginable; indeed, as already stated above in substance, in the elements of driving and sailing, the Vineyard stands almost unrivalled.

Away in the southernmost part of the island is the wonderful "Gay Head," brought into so unpleasant prominence a few years since by the wreck of the "City of Columbus" upon a ledge just off its shores. This headland is one of the most remarkable natural curiosities of New England, being composed of alternating strata of differently colored clays, red, white, yellow, green, etc., succeeding each other from base to summit, and displaying in the sunlight the most singular effects.

The outlooks from stand-points in this neighborhood are inexpressibly grand, whether over land or sea, and some of the most rugged of ocean features are included in every scene. In all the southern sections of the island, bird shooting and fishing are favorite pastimes, to be engaged in with certainty of sport. The bathing facilities of the island are also excellent in every part. Like all the region of south-eastern Massachusetts, Martha's Vineyard furnishes the foundation and location for many a legend and tradition, and these are quaintly set forth by the local oracles in terms always interesting.

A feature of Vineyard summer employments are the great fêtes, "illuminations," and the like, which take place from time to time during the evenings of the season. The island life in the villages is very animated while the warm months last, and the assemblages are made up of popular representatives from every section and country. Music and entertainment of every reasonable and seasonable kind abound, and the natural stimulation of the health-giving influences of the place renders all sojourners active partakers in the constant round of enjoyments. Indeed, the evenings at Martha's Vineyard are "superb," and there is no section where more complete recreation takes place or more desirable results are attained by the tired "vacationist" than on this lovely island.

Parties from New York, or the South and West, may reach Martha's Vineyard via New Bedford, and the sail between the two points, of from thirty to forty miles, is one of the finest afforded on the coast. The harbor of New Bedford within and without is exceedingly fine in point of scenery ; and the trip along the southern coasts, and especially for the last few miles before touching at Wood's Holl, is extremely interesting. Visitors from Boston and the North usually embark for the Vineyard at Wood's Holl, although they may make the trip via New Bedford if they so choose, the Old Colony Railroad furnishing equally desirable transportation to either point, and the connecting boats touching at both places. The Nantucket boats also make landings at the Vineyard at every trip, and the whole region is bound together and placed in constant communication by the Old Colony system, as completely as though the whole were one great family estate, managed and cared for by most beneficent care-takers.

NANTUCKET.

THE great beauty and attractiveness of the islands which lie off the shores of south-eastern Massachusetts long since make them famous among American summer resorts. Nantucket and Martha's Vineyard, Naushon and Pennikeese, and the multitude of lesser isles which dot the waters about Buzzard's Bay, or picket the south coasts — all these present in summer inducements for the attention of the tourist or recreation seeker which have no superior, and many which cannot be duplicated elsewhere. Nantucket! The name has been known for generations, it may now be said for centuries, in every part of the United States, and has always been synonymous with and suggestive of glorious summer pastimes.

Only thirty miles from the main-land, and dropped down like a beautiful haven of rest into the midst of the broad Atlantic, it has proved to be in very truth such a haven during every year of its known existence. Here one may turn his back upon the busy world and its vast concerns as effectually as though he had buried himself in an inland wilderness. Here every condition of life in summer is health-giving and recreative, and is held in conjunction with the finest opportunities for rational enjoyments. Physicians are agreed that for nervous, consumptive or hard-worn people, no locality offers better inducements for recuperation than does Nantucket in summer; while sound and hearty humanity, rejoicing in strength, and finding healthful excitement and zeal in natural provision and condition, declares that Nantucket has not its equal when the grass is green and summer breezes are fanning.

Only on the rarest occasions does the mercury reach so high a point on this island as 90° during the hottest of summer weather, and many years are noted during which 85° or 86° marked the greatest heat of any one day. The great water surfaces and the constant evaporation going forward on every hand here, causes a never-failing succession of breezes blowing over the land; and these come laden with the peculiar perfumes and influences which have so potent effects upon humanity, especially upon those representatives who ordinarily live far away from these conditions, and to whom they are a novelty and in the nature of life-giving medicines. Such persons are often able to note the good effects of these sanitary provisions from the very first hour of their coming among them; and the results of recreation and physical reform come to them as easily and as naturally as do the ministrations of Nature in any form or manifestation. In Nantucket there is no malaria, nor can there be any such thing under its "make-up." The sea-breezes blowing constantly across the island carry off every vestige of noxious gases or impure influences; and, as has already been hinted, the extremes of heat and cold are never so marked as to become disturbing elements in the sanitarium.

The principal village is furnished artificially with the purest water, drawn from an unfailing spring-fed pond; so that the two grand conditions of pure air and pure water are entirely met here. Other peculiarities are especially noted as belonging to the sanitarium of Nantucket: persons sojourning here invariably find the appetite and the inclination to sleep largely increased during their visits; showing both the tonic and sedative qualities of the air. And it has been clearly decided that the benefits to health here received are permanent, and to be carried away and enjoyed by the recipient wherever he may go. For countless thousands of city denizens, tired and worn by the ceaseless round of life at high pressure, it will be sufficient recommendation of this place as a summer resort that here one may be sure of finding cool nights for sleeping, and never a mosquito to hum his lullaby.

Within a few years there has happened a period when upwards of one-ninth of the population of the island was over seventy years old. During one recent year there were seventy-seven deaths in the place; and of this number, seventy-two per cent lived to the average of seventy-three years. Five of these deaths were of persons over ninety years of age; fifteen had lived over eighty years, and eighteen over seventy years. There were but eleven deaths of the number under thirty-six years of age, and of the eleven, seven were babes under one year old. The remaining ages were one of one year old, one of sixteen, and two of twenty-five. Surely there must be something "life-giving" in the sanitary condition of this island, to prolong existence and lower the death-rate according to this showing. The permanent population during that year was about 3,700.

It would be little to the purpose of this writing to discuss the problem of the primitive creation of this island in the midst of the sea; how the materials which enter into its "moraine" formation were gathered from the coasts of Labrador, the sides and surfaces of the White Mountains, and how what is now New England territory contributed generally and generously of fragments, which, carried during the glacial period in the grip of enormous icebergs and floes, were finally deposited where to this day they form the foundation of so many delights. The public can — and will — readily accept the theories of the scientists in these regards, as also in attestation of the fact that the gently rolling elevations now dignified by the title of "hills," found here and there upon the Nantucket surface, were once mountainous heights, many hundreds of feet above the ordinary level, and nodding in their grandeur to other and similar upheavals which stood in majesty near by, or where now, and for many centuries past, the Atlantic has rolled its waters without check or hindrance. It is sufficient for the ordinary summer visitor that the Nantucket of the present really exists, and has lost nothing in all the centuries of feature, condition or attribute which could better its ministrations as he finds them.

SANKATY HEAD LIGHT,
NANTUCKET.

THERE IS SOCIETY WHERE
NONE INTRUDES
BY THE DEEP SEA
AND MUSIC IN ITS
ROAR.

OLD MILL
NANTUCKET

NANTUCKET

NANTUCKET LIGHT.

R. NANTUCKET.

The once peculiar business features of Nantucket have disappeared. The pioneer in the whaling interests of this country, it formerly owned upwards of 300 vessels, many of them ships, devoted to that industry, and its wharves and docks were scenes of never-ceasing activity and enterprise. Those were the days when the "Long Tom Coffins," and the unique characters which have distinguished her history and illustrated her peculiarities, were in the height of their careers, and the contributions of Nantucket to the marine annals and literature of the world are indeed characteristic and to the last degree interesting. The flavor and the coloring of these early prosperous days and their pursuits still remain; but the glory of the place as an aggressive, executive community, with ways and methods of its own originating and interests carved out and managed for itself, have departed. No square-rigged vessel — hardly, indeed, a vessel of any kind — now lies at its wharves; and only the fortunes, or their remnants, the manners and customs, and the remarkable traits which distinguished her people during that famous period, are observable in the Nantucket life of to-day.

But the island has not changed, no more than have the frank, hearty, high-toned elements which have always characterized its population. Indeed, the dreamy, quiet, conservative conditions which now obtain in every part, have perhaps contributed more towards making this place the famous watering-place it has become, than her citizens would be willing to allow. The absence of the rush and whirl of competitive business operations, the free devotion of every natural feature and facility and advantage of the island to the interests of the summer sojourner and pleasure-seeker, the union of relations between the residents and the tourist and visitor in these directions, have done more in developing those conditions which in conjunction result in the finest and most desirable summering establishments, than could possibly have been wrought otherwise. For now both the permanent population and the transient residents are at one in making the most of every natural provision for summer enjoyments, and the main business of Nantucket, on the part of all concerned in her existence, is to make of her situation a garden of delights.

And in what place elsewhere are such delights to be found, or where else have any in their category been distributed with so lavish hand? So many of them, indeed, are inherent or peculiar to this island, and of those which exist in other localities nearly all are so greatly enhanced here, that Nantucket stands "alone in its glory" as the Queen of summering-places.

From the time when the Norsemen visited the place in the 11th century Nantucket has always been an island gem in ocean setting. Whatever of change and revolution may have taken place among the peoples which have from time to time occupied its territory, always this isle of the sea must have presented the same attractive and winsome features as at present. Between thirty and forty miles from the main-land, according to starting-point, this scrap of the world has offered itself to succeeding generations a haven of refuge and rest and peace; and now, as never before, do these attributes appear conspicuous to those who seek its shores, and their number is multiplying with marvellous rapidity.

It sometimes happens in winter that weeks go by without the possibility of passing to or from its shores. Its population is not increased, nor has it ever been, by adventurers or "roughs," or by discordant elements from varying climes and nationalities. The restless, scheming excitement-seeker or wrong-doer finds nothing attractive here; nor does the dead-beat, the hotel thief or sneak, and the rogue that preys upon society generally, care to operate in a place where he cannot slip away o'nights, and where the surroundings are ever too straitened for his lines of "business." This is the paradise for women and children, and men seeking rest and quiet and recreation through contact with Nature best disposed for these ends. White-winged, or stately moving steam, yachts animate the offing on every hand, and flit silently to or from haven and anchorage and mooring, their companies adding a constantly shifting and always welcome element by day or evening to circles wherein courtesy and noble bearing and refined intercourse are not occasional features, but the rule of life. Old Ocean offers here all that can ever characterize her best ministrations for humanity, and whether one whiles away the hours in boating, bathing, fishing or watching the various ocean moods from shore or headland, always the entertainment furnished is superlative—the very best possible under the conditions of the union of land and sea.

Most men who recognize at all the element of "sport" in fishing are agreed that for unalloyed enjoyment, free from dangerous or annoying features, bluefishing takes the palm, uniting as it does the very finest and most exciting elements of fishing and boating. For this pastime, and others like it, Nantucket seems to have been especially formed and dropped down where she is, there being no stint to the room or any qualification necessary to the perfection of the sport in the season. And this, indeed, may be said with regard to all kinds of fishing incidental to ocean or its shores, the fresh waters of Nantucket ponds and lakelets being included in the category of "advantages." The range of sea game here pursued includes varieties from diminutive perch to sharks, swordfish, and all that the waters of the latitude can furnish, and there is very little of "toiling all night and catching nothing" in the region of Nantucket.

But bluefishing, as has been said, is indeed the king of ocean sports. The rendezvous, where the company is select and sympathetic, and anticipation and expectancy form of themselves keen enjoyments; the boat, clean-heeled, swift, staunch, and fitted to a nicety for the service she is to perform; the start, the first heeling over gunwale deep before the breeze, which promises to keep at least one individual busy in the stern-sheets for the trip; the incidental measuring of speed and qualities with other craft onward bound, each crew intending to be "high line" for the day, if pluck and energy can assist performance; the getting down to business; the first throw; the first bite; the first fish landed under the thwarts; think you the evolutions of a naval battle, or the pursuit and capture of a pirate in the Yellow Sea, were ever half so satisfactorily exciting?

Unlike the rocky shores of the Isles of Shoals and many other resorts along the coast, Nantucket abounds in the finest bathing beaches, the white sands stretching away for miles often, the north shores especially sloping gradually into the roadstead, and having no dangerous undertow or other objectionable attributes. The near proximity of the Gulf Stream to the island has great influence in tempering the water, which, although the place is situated well out in the midst of the Atlantic, is deliciously agreeable to the bather of every condition. In the July days a temperature of at least 74° is pretty sure to characterize the waters about Brandt Point shores, and after

THE OLD VILLAGE PUMP AT SIASCONSET.

every rainfall, or muggy, misty period, these are particularly inviting. Indeed, so exceptionally desirable are the bathing facilities in this section, that the shore sloping backward and outward from Brandt Point toward the jetty is known as the "bathing beach." Brandt Point stands at the entrance of the ancient harbor, the channel, which must be traversed by all inbound vessels, running close in to the beach, as the point is neared, and making a bold, circular sweep around it as the inner harbor is gained.

It is an evidence of the estimation in which the bathing facilities of this beach are held that the "Nantucket," the latest acquisition to the number of Nantucket hotels, has a bathing-house of 100 rooms, while private bathing-houses are scattered all about, as if to make the most of the recreating influences. Nantucket has this commendation of its value as a summering-place, that its hotels are all excellent; but the Nantucket is the only one among them situated upon the shore; and already its proprietor, who is also mine host of the Ocean House at

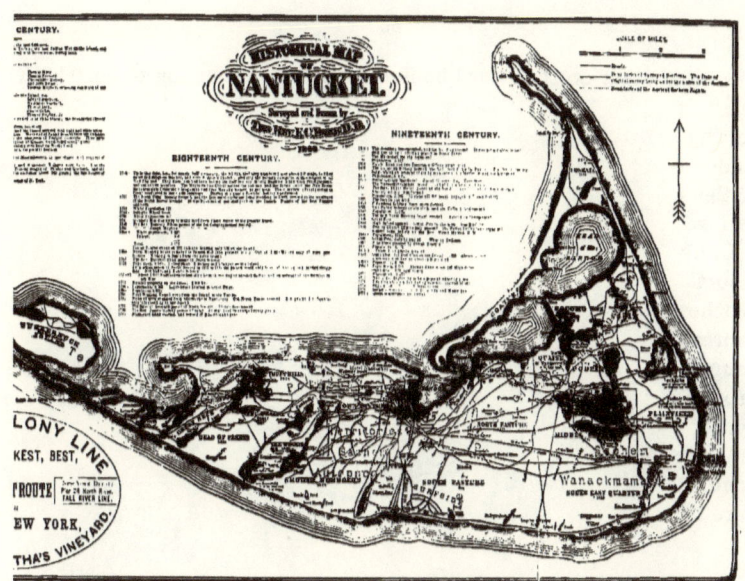

ities with other craft onward bound, each crew intending to be "high
line" fc
getting
landed ι
or the ι
half so
Unlik
resorts
beaches
shores ι
dangerε
proxim
pering
midst o
conditi
sure to

every
Indeeι
tion, ι
towar
stand:
be tra
the pι
inner
It i
this ɩ
numb
priva
of th
value
Nant
alrea(

the heart of the town, finds that he must double its size to accommodate all who would profit by his enterprise.

The surf bathing of the island can be found only at 'Sconset and Wauwinet, the beaches above referred to being found in the various indentations of the shore, or so nearly enclosed by peculiar coast formation that anything like a surf-line is precluded.

Nantucket is reached by steamboats, the sailing ports on the mainland being New Bedford and Wood's Holl, termini of Old Colony Railroad lines, and intermediate landing-places being at different points on Martha's Vineyard. The distances are: from New Bedford sixty miles, Wood's Holl thirty-four miles, and from Oak Bluffs (Martha's Vineyard) twenty-eight miles. The nearest point of outside land is Cape Pogc, twenty-one miles away, and Hyannis is twenty-seven miles distant. That portion of the course which lies between Martha's Vineyard and Nantucket furnishes an ocean trip, there being no land for thousands of miles eastward and southward except the island itself, which forms no appreciable check to the rolling billows as they obey the impulse of every breeze and storm. The trip from New Bedford to Wood's Holl, however, and from the last-named station to Martha's Vineyard, is along beautiful shores and among island scenery unequalled on the coast for attractions. Thrice daily during the summer season the islands are visited by the steamers, and mails and passengers have seldom to wait for transportation; never, in fact, unless some terrible storm is raging, or some such unforeseen natural cause interferes to defeat the plans. The Old Colony service, which includes in its management the great steamers of the Sound Line between Fall River, Newport and New York, has these southern coast lines also within its supervision and direction; and whether on sea or land the service of this system goes regularly forward, according to the dictates and teachings of years of experience in every branch, with no "hitch" in management or stay in methods.

The hotels and boarding-houses of Nantucket also form together a most significant feature among its desirable qualities. The latest comer on their list, "The Nantucket," alluded to above, is built fronting the beach just before Brandt Point is rounded, and its peculiar situation and modern style of architecture renders it one of the notable points long before the island is reached. Besides this, there are in the neighborhood of a dozen public hotels on the island, usually well kept and prepared for guests of every quality. The number of boarding-houses, and of private families which in summer devote their surplus rooms and best attentions to guests from abroad, is very large, and the excellent accommodations thus afforded are much appreciated by travellers and summer seekers. The fact that, compared with the practices which obtain at most of the average watering-places along the coasts, the cost of summering here seems insignificant, will without doubt have weight with many persons, who do not care to expend the earnings of a year for a month's summering, no matter what may be its advantages or enjoyments.

But perhaps the quaintest place on the Atlantic coast is the little village of Siasconset on the southeast corner of the island. Since 1880, it has become popular as a seaside resort. The village is venerable. It had its beginning two hundred years ago in rude cabins built by fishermen from Nantucket, for shelter at night, and when gales were blowing during the season for cod fishing in the spring and fall. By a process of slow evolution, these rudimentary dwellings were added to, now in this direction and then in that, as more room and greater comforts were required, and until a hundred years ago they had assumed about their present shape; and others begun at periods later were modeled after those completed. They are of fantastic shapes, but compact and strong and have withstood the storms of generations. They are huddled in close together, and in some instances are not more than five feet apart, and the little by-ways between them are dignified as streets, with pretentious names, though some are scarce fifty feet long. There are less than fifty of these ancient fishermen's cottages. All are shingled down their sides as well as on their roofs. The ridge poles in some are only ten or eleven feet high, while the eaves of the additions used for bed-rooms are sometimes not more than four or five feet from the ground. Broad chimnies, built when coal for fuel had not been dreamed of for the Islanders, project through roofs, in marked disproportion to the size of the dwellings. When one enters the cottages it becomes apparent that they were designed and built by sailors. Parlor, bed-room and closet, suggest cabin, stateroom and locker. The little attic, if there be one, is reached by a ladder or almost perpendicular stair that looks like the companionway from a ship's cabin. The furniture is of odds and ends brought from Nantucket, and all is ancient except the modern stove which has replaced the big primitive fireplace. These little cottages are occupied each season by families of intelligence, refinement and even of wealth, from our large cities, who rent them from their owners, and find in them comfort and enjoyment for the season. But since 1880 over seventy-five houses have been erected, some for the use of their owners, and others to let furnished to summer visitors. Some are of pretentious architecture, but a New York gentleman who became enamored of life in the old cottages has built nearly a score of others in the ancient style, only making them more commodious and furnishing them with modern appliances for the comfort and convenience of tenants. He rents them at low rates and has found his investment profitable.

'Sconset (as the natives call the place) is situated on a bluff, before which is a beach three hundred feet in width. With the surf almost at their doors visitors daily avail themselves of the opportunity afforded to wrestle with the billows, and the beach is fringed with a line of tents and awnings under which young and old rest during pleasant days until the season is about to close.

The village is a paradise for children, and a haven of rest for invalids, wearied brain-workers, and tired-out business men.

BUZZARD'S BAY — ONSET, AND
ALONG SHORE.

HE sail across the outer portion of Buzzard's Bay, in making the trip by steamer from New Bedford to Wood's Holl, Martha's Vineyard and Nantucket, has more than once been referred to in these pages. The waters of Buzzard's Bay wash more of beautiful shores than can be found upon any other section of United States coast from Maine to Georgia; and if the islands included in the locality are taken into account, upwards of a half-hundred miles of the finest marine situations imaginable are here outspread. The waters of this bay make frequent incursions inland, and have hollowed out for themselves in the course of time, deep indentations in the shore-line, and thread among the islands and headlands in the most fantastic manner, breaking the coasts into the most variegated scenes. Whether one begins the traversing of these shores from the New Bedford or the Wood's Holl termini, all the same he finds successions of the finest beaches and the fairest combination of land and water scenery. The boundaries of many towns—Falmouth, Wareham, Marion, Mattapoisett, Fairhaven — are included in these distances, and many spots have become famous for their natural beauties or advantages and the varied attractions they present to the tourist, the pleasure seeker or the summer sojourner. The bay itself is full of charms for the visitor, aside from the natural attributes of which it is possessed. Within its waters many varieties of the finest fish afford superior sporting facilities in connection with boating; upon its surface in many parts there is rare sport in gunning in its season; some of the finest oysters known in ocean or river waters are found within its upper sections; and here the pursuit of game fish acquires a zest and a satisfactory quality which few localities present or can equal.

The beaches on the eastern side of this bay, or between Wood's Holl and the Wareham boundary, are of the very finest description. Of the number, Monument Beach is perhaps the most attractive, while all are destined within a short time in the future to become famous, and much sought by summer visitors. Already along these shores some of the most noted private summering establishments of the whole coast are to be found; and many of these vie with the shore estates of Newport in the lavish provision and outlay in their planting.

So numerous have lately become the summer residents of wealth and social position in this quarter, that a special train-service has been instituted for their use by the Old Colony Railroad management, which enterprise deserves passing mention in this connection. The "Dude" train, as this provision is euphoniously entitled, runs between Boston

FALMOUTH VILLAGE.

BEACH VIEW.

YACHTING

VIEWS ALONG BUZZARDS BAY.

QUISSETT HARBOR AND HOTEL FALMOUTH.

and Wood's Holl every summer, from June 1 to October 1, and is emphatically the summer residents' service. The train is made up entirely
of drawing-room cars, and no person is admitted to ride upon it who is
not of the association of passengers who charter it, or their friends
whom they may invite to join them on a trip. Any resident of the
section, however, may become a member of this association and make
use of the train, by paying the regular passenger fare and the bonus
for the season demanded for its provision. No stop is made between
Boston and Wareham going either way, and below Wareham stops are
made only at Buzzard's Bay and Falmouth. Possibly Monument Beach
may be added to the stations at which calls are made the present
season. This train averages never less than fifty miles an hour in its
running; and, allowing for time lost in making stops, it frequently
attains a speed of sixty miles per hour for the trip — a running time
not excelled by any passenger line in the world. Every facility is
afforded the passenger for comfort and convenience. Newspapers are
taken on at Brockton without stopping, on the up trip in the morning,
and a fine smoking-car is provided. The train is very popular with its
patrons, and they constantly delight in its performances.

Immediately inland from the eastern and northern shores of Buzzard's
Bay are the grand old Falmouth, Sandwich and Plymouth woods, where
numerous deer still range, and primeval scenes extend for miles un-
broken by the innovations of humanity. These woods are filled with
the finest ponds, some of which are fairly lakes, and winding roads
traverse them in every part, inviting to driving excursions even as the
waters of the bay invite to fairest sailing trips. Indeed, the alternation
of land and water delights and pastimes is a principal feature of the
locality for summer sojourning, and every taste for out-door employments or enjoyments can here be satisfied.

Off the lower Wareham shore a deep indentation of the bay receives
the name of "Onset," and this section has now become widely known
as the encamping-place of the Spiritualists during the summer heats,
and where their "meetings" are held in the same way that the Wesley-
ans utilize Martha's Vineyard. Thousands of persons frequently arrive
at Onset on a single day during the season, and already the place has
a "cottage city" of its own, and is growing in population and summer
institutions and establishments beyond all precedent. And well indeed
it may, for no spot on all the coasts can surpass this for natural attractions. The bay about is dotted with islands, which shelter the main-
land, as it were, and divide the water surface into straits and passages
and sheltered coves. The shores are alternating sand beaches and
bouldered reaches, and gently swelling hills recede inland from these,
crowned with woods growth which often comes down to the very
water's edge. Here is a paradise for women and children; and many
people, who have perhaps not the slightest interest in the sectarian
attractions of the place, have now chosen it for summer residence on
account of its superlative natural features, the situation being enhanced

by the developing and utilizing agency of the "Association" (Spiritualists) which has assumed its management. The bathing facilities here are especially fine, the children tumbling about in the miniature surf with rarest enjoyment. The sailing and fishing advantages are of the best.

Along the shores of the bay westward there are constantly recurring little nooks and sheltered localities, the perfect abodes of restful quiet and recreative influences during the summer days, and the fairest exponents of fine land and water scenes as they exist only in New England.

At intervals all along this shore persons of wealth, having noted the great beauties and natural endowments of the section, have fixed their summer abodes, and the whole region is now developing and occupying in the most satisfactory manner. From the Marion and Mattapoisett shores and the elevations that border upon them the finest water views are obtained, while the forest growth of those sections in the immediate vicinity has always attracted attention by its luxuriousness and great extent.

Still further westward the New Bedford shores and surroundings are enchanting through the fine scenes they present, and in no section are fairer advantages for summering offered. Between Mattapoisett and New Bedford a beautifully variegated shore stretches along, from which the Elizabeth Islands — Cuttyhunk, Pasque, Naushon — may be studied or visited. Along these shores the Nantucket and Vineyard steamers skirt, and the waters about here swarm with finest fish, bass, bluefish, scup, squeteague, etc., or the sport may be enlarged by systematic hunting for the more ponderous sword-fish. The islands in this vicinity are generally private property, well kept and stocked, and always objects of interest to all comers.

From New Bedford still westward to Newport — Buzzard's Bay having been passed — only a continuation of these fair scenes is presented. On these last-named shores the denizens of New Bedford and Fall River, and the more inland towns of that part of New England lying contiguous, congregate during the warm months, and here the features which distinguish the Newport shores largely attain. In short, this whole region, now rapidly "making up," has been endowed naturally with summer attractions second to none on the coasts, with sanitary and health-giving influences not surpassed in the country; and it is now fast growing in the estimation of all travellers, as it has for many decades existed with those who were fortunate enough to know of its merits.

⟶❖ HERE AND THERE. ❖⟵

It must not be concluded, because of the space accorded to the description of seashore points in this little volume, that the Old Colony system traverses no inland sections, ministers to no rural or country localities, which may be made the desirable resorts of the "summer-seeker." On the contrary, south-eastern and eastern Massachusetts excels nearly every other section of New England in this regard, and the railroad referred to runs its lines through some of the most delightful inland scenes and situations extant. Many persons prefer to sojourn a few miles inland from the coast, from whence the shore is easily reached and ocean delights may be made available at will, while village life and country associations form the centre of the recreative excursion. To such, the in-shore towns and hamlets of the Old Colony and its neighborhood offer superior advantages, its territory being favored far beyond most sections in all the elements of fine natural scenery, excellent sanitary conditions, diversity of situation and employments afforded, and facilities for summer pastimes and enjoyments, and the quality of its population and community "make-up." Its farming sections are more beautiful, and more complete in every requisite and attribute for summer-sojourning, than often happens in any region; and the great advantages afforded by an old settled country, with communities contiguous and sympathetic, are here apparent in every part. No finer rural inland resorts can be found anywhere than the Bridgewaters, Abingtons, Middleboro', Marion, and the like places in the south-eastern sections, and in nearly every part of the Northern Division of the Old Colony Railroad, and especially Northboro', Southboro', Framingham, Leominster, Berlin, Acton, Chelmsford, and the rest. Scattered through all these sections and communities are to be found grand old estates and families, the finest exponents of cottage life, and such fancy or special farming establishments as no other region can equal, — besides the usual manifestations of a farming section of notable quality. But here, as along the seashore, the superlative natural attributes of the section are constantly apparent, and these furnish of themselves its strongest attractions for visitors from every quarter. During the summer months, sojourners are accordingly present by thousands, and the whole region is made animate by the constant manifestation of this presence in every department of rural and town life. In short, the combination of seashore and inland enjoyments which distinguishes the Old Colony system is most superior in every regard.

Following is indicated the location and attributes of the principal localities along the Old Colony lines, in addition to those already referred to in foregoing pages : —

WOLLASTON HEIGHTS,

An elevated site, charmingly located on the south shore of Massachusetts Bay, and one of the most beautiful of the many attractive villages in this locality. Overlooking Boston's magnificent harbor, with its scores of islands, and every passing steamer in full view, it has become a favorite spot for homes.

QUINCY.

This old town is rich in historical incidents, and noted as the birthplace and residence of men eminent in the early history of our country. Years before her granite hills were laid open to supply materials for the foundations and walls of our public edifices, she gave to the nation some of the chief corner-stones in the history of our Republic. John Adams, the second President of the United States, and John Hancock, the first signer of the Declaration of Independence, were born and died in this town. It is also the birthplace of John Quincy Adams, our sixth President, and of Edmund Quincy. Few towns in the State are so rich in Revolutionary memories as this. Some of the buildings, relics of those ancient days, are still standing, and well worth examining, among which are the venerable houses in which Hannah Adams and John Quincy Adams were born. The former is near the railroad on the left, in passing southward, and the latter near Penn's Hill. The railroad stations are at Atlantic, Wollaston Heights, Quincy, and Quincy Adams. Other sections of the town are known as Quincy Point and Squantum.

BRAINTREE,

On the south of Quincy, the principal villages of which are Braintree, ten miles, and South Braintree, eleven miles from Boston, on the main line of the Old Colony Railroad, is an old and interesting town. From some of its more elevated portions delightful prospects of the ocean are obtained. In the southern section are two beautiful ponds; one of some one hundred and fifty acres, known as Great Pond, and the other, Cranberry Pond, of twenty-five acres. Both of these are well stocked with fish.

HANSON,

Like Abington, divides its waters in an easterly and a westerly direction. Indian Head Pond sends a stream into the North River, which finds its way to the ocean on the eastern shore; while Poor-meadow Brook enters the Satucket River in East Bridgewater, and the latter, uniting with the Wenetuxet in Halifax, forms the Taunton River.

HALIFAX,

A fine old town, twenty-five miles from Boston by rail, was originally settled by the descendants of the Pilgrims. Monponset Pond and other large sheets of fresh water are favorite resorts for fishing and gunning; while the surrounding forests, of which there are over two thousand acres, afford game of various kinds, and attract many sportsmen.

PLYMPTON

Is twenty-nine miles from Boston by the Old Colony Railroad, which passes through the north village, a pleasant location on Silver Lake. Wenetuxet Village is on a beautiful stream of the same name, which flows into the Taunton River. The town abounds in forests of oak, maple, pine and cedar. The several villages afford excellent opportunities to families desiring a retired and pleasant summer retreat. Here are large picnic grounds belonging to the Old Colony Railroad.

KINGSTON

Was early settled by members of the Pilgrim band. Gov. Bradford and his sons made their residence here, which was then a portion of the town of Plymouth. Like other towns in this vicinity, Kingston has lakes and fresh-water streams in abundance.

HOLBROOK,

Fifteen miles from Boston on the Old Colony Railroad, is situated on elevated land, the water-shed between the Massachusetts and Mount Hope bays. The Cochato River receives its waters on the north, and Beaver River on the south. Its elevated site renders it one of the most healthy localities in Southern Massachusetts, and affords from its prominent points some enchanting views.

BROCKTON,

The only city in Plymouth County, is twenty miles from Boston by the Old Colony Railroad. Two brooks — Trout and Salisbury — unite within limits of the city, in the eastern portion, forming the Salisbury River, whose waters mingle with the Taunton in Halifax.

Brockton has a population of 20,000, engaged principally in the manufacture of shoes, shoe tools, dies, patterns, lasts, and forms, sewing-machine needles, furniture, etc., and is the centre of trade for the adjacent territory.

There is a street railway some four miles in length, connecting the city proper with Campello; and ten lines of coaches radiate to the towns around.

Campello, "a plain," is a village in the southern portion of Brockton, where there is also a station on the Old Colony Railroad.

THE BRIDGEWATERS.

Bridgewater is an agricultural town. The surface of the land is somewhat diversified by hill and valley, but generally level. Nippenicket Pond, in the western part, is a beautiful sheet of water of three hundred and eighty acres, and studded with islands. The Taunton River, formed by a union of the Wenetuxet, Matfield and Town Rivers, divides the town on its southern border from Middleboro'. It is twenty-seven miles from Boston by rail.

East Bridgewater was set off from Bridgewater in 1823. It is generally a manufacturing town, though partly agricultural, and is abundantly watered by numerous rivers and brooks. Robbins Pond, of one hundred and thirty acres, is in the southern portion of the town.

West Bridgewater is largely agricultural. It was originally a portion of Bridgewater, being separated in 1822.

MIDDLEBORO',

Thirty-four miles from Boston on the Old Colony Railroad, is largely devoted to manufacturing. There is still considerable woodland within the town. It is watered by the Taunton, Mattapoisett and Weweantit rivers. Within its borders is a beautiful sheet of water of about one hundred and eighty acres, called Wood's Pond.

On that branch of the Old Colony Railroad leading from Middleboro' towards Fall River, and two and a half miles from the former place, is

LAKEVILLE,

So named because of the extensive and beautiful chain of lakes lying mostly within its border. This locality is rapidly becoming one of our attractive summer resorts. Assawamsett Pond, three by five miles in extent, surrounded by forests and cultivated fields, is one of the most romantic localities to be found in New England. Its waters abound in all the native varieties of fish, together with the land-locked salmon and black bass. There is a steamer on the lake capable of accommodating upwards of seventy passengers, together with a fleet of sail and row boats for pleasure and fishing. Connected with the Assawamsett, as knees and arms and elbows, are Long Pond, one mile wide by seven miles long, Pocsha Pond, and the Great and Little Quitticus, — the three latter united being equal in extent to the Assawamsett. These waters abound in different varieties of fish, and afford facilities for extended excursions.

On the borders of the Assawamsett are two picnic groves, one at Stony Point and the other at Green Point, furnished with cook-houses and small cottages designed mainly for transient parties. Excellent opportunities are afforded in the vicinity of these ponds for families or clubs who desire to camp out for a season. The forests bordering on these lakes still abound in game.

WAREHAM,

At the head of Buzzard's Bay, is forty-nine miles from Boston. The surface of the town is exceedingly level, and sand abounds in all directions. Notwithstanding its unfavorable appearance in this respect, it is a favorite resort of sportsmen. The numerous ponds and streams afford a great variety of fresh-water fish, while the inlets and harbor, and especially Wareham Narrows, supply blue-fish, tautog, bass, sea-perch and sea-trout in their season. The harbor is on the Waukinco River, and has a depth of ten to fifteen feet of water. On the west is Weweantit, and on the east the Agawam River.

SANDWICH.

Just where Cape Cod curves outward from the main coast on the Massachusetts Bay shore, lies Sandwich, properly the first town on the Cape. It is about sixty miles from Boston, on the Cape Division of the Old Colony Railroad.

The surface of the land is generally undulating, presenting many beautiful slopes and elevated sites. It deserves especial mention as combining comfort and pleasure with moderate expense and ease of access to those seeking abiding-places through the heated term.

There are about thirty thousand acres of woodland, dotted with beautiful miniature lakes; and, to the delight of the sportsman, abounding in game,—from the graceful deer to the velvet-footed hare and whirring partridge. The sparkling, pebbly-bottomed trout streams are pleasantly associated with reminiscences of Webster's fishing days; while the wide, open marshes, clean-swept daily by Old Ocean, fill the air with delicious, salty fragrance—invigorating with new life the weary, debilitated invalid,—and in their season filled with the various game-birds of the North. Excellent facilities are offered for boating, bathing and fishing.

MONUMENT BEACH,

On the western shores of Sandwich, at the eastern head of Buzzard's Bay and near the mouth of Monument River, is destined at no distant day to be ranked among our first-class watering-places. Already it has an excellent hotel, and summer cottages are rapidly accumulating. The beach is hard and smooth, and affords excellent opportunities for bathing. From Monument Beach, a boat-sail to Burgess Point, a distance of about a mile and a half, or across to Marion, some six miles, or along the eastern shore, can scarcely be equalled. The bay is studded with gems of beauty.

FALMOUTH.

As a quiet place of rest and recreation, Falmouth has few rivals on our coast. Situated on a promontory forming the extreme southern point of the town is Wood's Holl—the southern terminus of this branch of the Old Colony Railroad, and a landing-place of the line of steamers to Martha's Vineyard and Nantucket. The harbor is a noted haven of safety for vessels in stress of weather. From Nobska Hill we have a charming view of the Sound, of the Vineyard shore, of Tisbury Hills, and of the Elizabeth Islands. From the same standpoint, looking northward across the neck of land, the whole stretch of Buzzard's Bay is before us.

The principal village of Falmouth, a beautiful hamlet nestling half a mile from the station, is near the crescent-shaped beach on the southern shore, which extends from the landing nearly to Nobska Lighthouse. About one mile from this village, in a southerly direction, is Falmouth Heights, one of the most delightful resorts bordering on Vineyard Sound, reached by carriage from Falmouth station on the Old Colony Railroad. Here we find, most emphatically, a fashionable watering-place combined with a delightful and inexpensive retreat for a summer's sojourn, a week's recreation, or a day's pastime. The scenery, whether maritime or inland, is romantic and charming. Southward is a marine highway, with its hundreds of moving objects—the white sails and the deep-laden steamers of commerce passing east and west; pleasure-boats innumerable skimming from headland to headland, or coasting from shore to shore; a white-hulled steamer of the Old Colony line is shooting out from Wood's Holl on our right or rounding East Chop on the opposite shore, and heading toward us. The view is grand, interesting and instructive. The hotel at the Heights is decidedly homelike and comfortable; and the place, owing to its excellent facilities for boating, bathing and other health-giving pastimes, is rapidly filling with summer cottages.

Menauhant, a new watering-place on the beach bordering on the Sound, with fine hotel, and already an excellent reputation. On turning from East Falmouth, the hotel stands in full view at a distance of two miles down the avenue, like a citadel guarding the approach to the beach. Menauhant (pronounced Menant) is connected with Wood's Holl and Falmouth Landing by a fairy-like steamer, affording a delightful sail of about five miles along the crescent-shaped shore of the Sound. From Menauhant, eastward by boat about two miles, is Waquoit Bay, entering which we find ourselves on a beautiful expanse of water, almost land-locked — the entrance being very narrow. Quashnet River, leading from John's Pond in Mashpee, enters the bay at Waquoit Village. Skirting the shore of the Sound still further eastward, we enter Popponessett Bay, into which flows the Mashpee River, — a beautiful stream of which Mashpee and Wakeby ponds are the source, — and Cotuit River, flowing from Santuit Pond. A sail of a few miles further eastward brings us to Cotuit Port. From many points along the shore we have fine views of Martha's Vineyard, especially from Succonessett Headland, an elevated site midway between Waquoit and Popponessett bays.

MASHPEE,

The Indian town lying between Falmouth and Barnstable, has a coast on Vineyard Sound extending from Waquoit Bay to Popponessett Bay, and an interior containing several Indian villages, numerous large and beautiful ponds, and woodlands and forests in which the red deer still range. It is an interesting district to visit, and easily reached by carriage, either from Falmouth on the Wood's Holl branch, or Sandwich, on the Cape Cod Division of the Old Colony Railroad; and pleasanter drives are nowhere to be found than those over the smooth roads tending shoreward or landward, along river banks, or circling the ponds throughout the town. These people live by agricultural pursuits, the manufacture of various articles of Indian ware, by the sale of their wood, and by fishing, fowling, and deer hunting. They are a docile and hospitable people, and the largest remnant of all the tribes of red men west of the Penobscot River, who, but a little more than two centuries ago, were fee-simple proprietors of the whole territory of New England.

BARNSTABLE,

The southern road passing through Cotuit, while those further inland carry us by way of Marston's Mills.

Cotuit Port is within the limits of Barnstable, and is also reached directly by carriage from the Old Colony Railroad station at West Barnstable. It was one of the first places on the Cape selected as a summer resort by city denizens. The main street is pleasantly shaded, and closely bordered by handsome cottages; among them the homes of sea captains who have made their native Cape famous for seamanship and Yankee enterprise. Off from the street, and approached by avenues through cultivated grounds, are numerous cottages and villas, — the summer residences of wealthy city dwellers, who early recognized the beauties of this retreat. The marine views from the promontory of the highlands, where the shore ends abruptly in a bold water-front, are among the finest on the coast; and the facilities for surf-bathing, fishing and boating are unexcelled. The village is frequented mostly by those who resort here year after year, and who have found in its seclusion and bracing atmosphere that quiet comfort and recuperation so much needed. Hotel and boarding-house accommodations are excellent, and moderate in price. From here to Osterville we find the same delightful drive; and here we would fain tarry in the comfortable apartments and at the bountiful board of the Cotocheset House, — a large summer hotel located near the beach on the Sound shore. From here we can again take a carriage for a drive to Hyannis, passing through Centreville, a charming village affording quiet, rest and recreation for the many city visitors who pass their summer vacation here. In this village is a small pond, noted for its rare *pink* water-lilies. Osterville and Centreville are both connected by carriages with the West Barnstable station on the Old Colony Railroad.

Hyannis (Indian *Iyanough*), named for a friendly Sachem, once the owner of the territory, is the most southerly village in Massachusetts, and is rapidly becoming a fashionable watering-place. Summer residences in "fantastic shapes and colors gorgeous" abound in every direction; and two large and excellent hotels — the Iyanough, at the station of the Hyannis branch of the Cape Cod Division, and the Hallet House, at Hyannis Port, offer good accommodations to one hundred and fifty summer boarders.

RANDOLPH.

This town was, until 1793, a part of Braintree, known as the South Parish. The Blue Hill River is its northern border. A portion of Great Pond is within the limits of Randolph, as is also a part of Punkapoag Pond. The principal village is beautifully located on elevated ground, a little to the west of which is Tower Hill; and from this point a fine prospect of the surrounding country is obtained. Boot and shoe manufacturing is the principal industry. It is fifteen miles from Boston by rail.

STOUGHTON

Is also largely engaged in the manufacture of boots and shoes. Two lines of the Old Colony Railroad pass through the town, one of which is the Stoughton station, nineteen miles from Boston, and on the other the East Stoughton station, seventeen miles.

EASTON.

This town is divided into three villages —North Easton, Easton and South Easton. The former is an exceedingly pleasant place, its churches and many of its private dwellings being built of a handsome stone peculiar to the locality. North Easton is noted for the extensive shovel manufactories of the Messrs. Oliver Ames & Sons Corporation, at whose works more than one-half of the shovels used on the continent are made. There are three beautiful sheets of fresh water in the town, — Wilbur's Pond, of some two hundred acres in extent; Ames Pond, two miles in length, and Flyaway Pond of seventy-five acres.

RAYNHAM.

Thirty miles from Boston by rail, and situated on the north of the Taunton River, is the old town of Raynham, whose early history is so full of exciting events of Indian wars and Indian life. King Philip's "summer residence" was on the banks of Fowling Pond, in the westerly section of the town. This pond was once the resort of the wild goose and other water fowl, but is now a mere swamp overgrown with pine and cedar. Nippenicket Pond is still a pleasant sheet of water.

TAUNTON

Is a beautiful and growing city on the river of the same name, thirty-four miles from Boston by the Old Colony Railroad. The streets are generally well shaded with large trees, and contain many fine residences and cultivated grounds. Its manufactures are extensive and varied. The Locomotive Works are among the most extensive of the kind in the country, covering many acres. There are also large and flourishing nail and tack manufactories. The Taunton River is here navigable, and rolls gracefully through the centre of the city.

The principal portion of Taunton was originally purchased from the Indians by Miss Elizabeth Pool, the consideration therefor being a coat, a few hatchets, and some beans. Miss Pool was a lady of considerable fortune, having left England, like others of the old Puritan stock, that she might enjoy the "religion of her conscience." She formed a settlement here for the purpose of converting Indians to Christianity.

DIGHTON

Is forty miles from Boston. The Old Colony Railroad passes along the margin of the Taunton River through the whole length of the town. From its elevation one of the most comprehensive views on the coast is obtained, extending from Mount Hope southward, to the Blue Hills northward. On Assonet Neck, on the opposite side of the river, in the town of Berkley, is the celebrated Dighton Rock, the origin of the inscriptions on which has long been a matter of dispute among antiquarians. The rock is eleven feet long and about five feet high. The inscriptions consist of outlines of human heads and bodies, interspersed with crosses and letters of curious formation.

FALL RIVER,

Called the "Border City," because of its situation on the line of Rhode Island, is forty-nine miles from Boston by rail. It is the eastern terminus of the celebrated Fall River Line of steamers, which, after touching at Newport, pass up the Bay to this point. It is a manufacturing city — the great New England city of spindles, beautifully located on Mount Hope Bay. Here the Providence and Warren Line of the Old Colony Railroad crosses the Taunton River on a magnificent iron bridge.

Nearly opposite Fall River, on the eastern shore of Bristol Neck, lies MOUNT HOPE, where King Philip held his Pokanoket court. From the summit of this mount we compass Rhode Island, and almost hold it like a bouquet in our hand. Nearly every city and town in the State is visible, while the islands in the bay are spread at our feet. Providence on our right, and Newport on the left, are in the distance; Warren and Bristol in the immediate foreground on either hand, and Warwick in front and more distant, with hamlets and villages interspersed.

Most travellers gain their first glimpse and impressions of Newport by approach from the Sound.

ATTLEBORO.

From Taunton, the junction of the Main Line and Northern Divisions, a branch road of eleven miles extends to Attleboro', a busy town, noted for its manufacture of jewelry. At this point the Boston & Providence Railroad intersects, affording direct connection with Providence and Pawtucket.

NORTON.

One of the prominent physical features of this town is its abundance of water. Rivers, brooks and streamlets abound in every direction, and there is a fine sheet of water known as Winnecunnet Pond, covering some one hundred and twenty-two acres in extent. On Rocky Hill is a cave formed by two large rocks, and still known as Philip's Cave. This was the abode of the Sachem while on his fishing excursions to Winnecunnet Pond and the neighboring streams, all of which still abound in pickerel. The Wheaton Female Seminary is located in Norton, ranking among the best institutions of the kind in New England.

MANSFIELD.

This old town, like Norton, is also well watered, and is, consequently, an attractive locality for knights of the rod. It contains several very pleasant ponds, stocked with perch and pickerel. Its central village is a busy and thriving place, with good railroad facilities and many handsome private residences. Mansfield is extensively engaged in the manufacture of stoves and ranges, and also of straw goods. At Mansfield the Northern Division of the Old Colony crosses the Boston & Providence Railroad.

FOXBORO'

Is a prosperous and pleasant town, with a fine park and a good hotel. Cocasset Pond and many of the beautiful streams are well stocked with perch and pickerel. The Neponset River, which rises in this town, flows in a northerly and easterly direction, while Billings Brook and Furnace Brook, two beautiful streams, flow southward, being tributaries of the Taunton. The manufacture of straw goods is one of the principal industries.

WALPOLE.

The Old Colony and the New York & New England Railroads intersect at this place. The south village is just half-way between Boston and Providence, on the old turnpike, and in the old days of stage travel was the stopping-place for dinner.

MEDFIELD

Is one of the old and famous historical towns of New England. The Charles River flows on its westerly border, on the banks of which its farms are well cultivated and exceedingly productive. It is situated on elevated ground, with a dry, gravelly soil, and is, consequently, a very healthy locality. From Castle Hill, Mount Nebo, Noon Hill and Rock Woods, there are fine landscapes and charming scenery.

At Medfield Junction, one and a half miles northward, the Woonsocket branch of the New York & New England Railroad crosses the tracks of the Old Colony. Near the station at the Junction is a beautiful picnic grove bordering on a pond. Two miles north of the Junction the railroad crosses the Charles River, the dividing line between the towns of Medfield and Sherborn, and also of the counties of Norfolk and Middlesex.

SHERBORN.

This is principally an agricultural town, in the midst of the great apple district of Massachusetts. There is a steam cider mill in the south village, the annual production of which is nearly twenty thousand barrels of refined cider. Sawin Academy is located on a beautiful eminence overlooking the town. Between Sherborn and South Framingham the railroad lies alongside of and crosses the new conduit of the Boston Water Works. For many miles at various points along this section, the traveller has views of conduits, dams, gate-houses and broad sheets of water, the results of the expenditure of millions of dollars in order to obtain a sufficient supply of water both for the present and prospective needs of the city of Boston.

FRAMINGHAM.

The surface of this delightful old town is generally level, or but slightly undulating, with the exception of Nobscot Hill in the north-west, Merriam's and Ballard's Hills in the south-west, and the beautiful hill in the central village, on which the State Normal School is located. The Sudbury River winds in a serpentine course through the Centre, where it is joined by Stony Brook. There are several beautiful ponds and lakes within the town, Cochituate Lake lying on the eastern border, and Shakum Pond, Learned Pond and Farm Pond (the latter much the larger of the four) in the southern section. Harmony Grove, on the eastern shore of Farm Pond, is a well-known and favorite resort for picnic parties, etc. South Framingham is one of the most important railroad centres in the State, being the junction of the Old Colony and Boston & Albany Railroads. Close connections are here made for Springfield, Albany and the West. The State Arsenal is located in this section of the town, as are also the Parade Grounds of the State militia, where the force is annually mustered for review and inspection in the months of August and September. While passing over Farm Pond, on the line of the railroad from the south to the central village, the tourist catches a glimpse of the Lake View Camp Ground, with its rustic cottages in the woods, on old Mount Walte. Lake View Station is in close proximity to the grove. The central village—its streets shaded with elms, maples and other varieties of ornamental trees, its stately mansions and magnificent roads—presents an air of elegance and repose.

At Framingham the Old Colony Railroad extends its arms in two directions—north-wardly towards the Merrimack, and northwesterly through the rich and fertile valleys to the heart of Worcester County, holding in its embrace much of the agricultural and manufacturing wealth of the State.

SUDBURY

Lies embosomed to-day in the same fertile meadows which afforded the favorite feeding grounds of the wild deer while yet the red man held undisputed sway over the "forest, the fish and the brute." In its early history Sudbury was noted for the abundance of game, both of forest and water, which only too frequently proved the cause of terrible and sanguinary conflicts between the two races. At Concord Junction, between Sudbury and Acton, the Old Colony intersects the Fitchburg Railroad.

ACTON

Comprises several villages, mostly farming districts. South Acton has various manufacturing industries. In the Centre are several handsome private residences of well-shaded streets. Here stands a granite monument erected to the memory of Captain Isaac Davis, killed in the fight at Concord Bridge, April 19, 1775.

CARLISLE AND CHELMSFORD

Are both agricultural districts, the productions of the [farm, garden and dairy finding a ready market in the city of Lowell.

LOWELL,

A northern terminus of the Old Colony Railroad, is one of the most flourishing manufacturing cities in New England, Pawtucket Falls on the Merrimac River furnishing an inexhaustible water-power. Its products of cotton cloth, carpets, machinery, etc., are sent to all parts of the world. At Lowell the Old Colony Railroad connects with the Boston & Maine, Boston & Lowell, Nashua & Lowell and Stony Brook Railroads, its New York trains making close connections with the great northern route to Manchester, Concord and the White Mountain regions.

SOUTHBORO'.

The northwestern arm of this division of the Old Colony Railroad intersects some of the finest agricultural towns and fruit-growing districts in Massachusetts. Southboro' is the first town on this arm of the road after leaving Framingham. It is classed among the pleasantest towns in the State. The centre, which is located on rising ground, commands an extensive prospect. The other villages are Fayville (in which there is a station), Cordaville and Southville.

MARLBORO'

Is reached by a spur track branching off the main road on the right a few miles above Southboro'. Although noted as rich in agricultural and horticultural wealth, its recent rapid growth and prosperity are largely owing to its extensive manufacture of boots and shoes.

NORTHBORO'

Is a valley town nestling between the high lands of Westboro' and Boylston, and only twelve miles distant from the city of Worcester. It is watered by the Assabet River, and from Assabet Hill, a beautiful eminence near the centre, the spires of some twenty churches may be seen in the surrounding towns. Northboro' is quite extensively known from the popular products of its excellent dairies.

BERLIN.

This town presents a somewhat rocky and hilly appearance. Gates Pond, in the eastern section, is well stored with fish, and many of the brooks afford good trout fishing.

BOLTON

Is a picturesque agricultural town, on an elevated situation of remarkable scenic beauty. Wattoquattoc Hill is the highest elevation between Boston and Wachusett Mountain, and from its summit the dome of the State House can be seen in clear weather.

Passing from Bolton, the railroad lies through the valley of the Nashua River, along which the panorama is exceedingly beautiful. The fertile river-meadows, hedged and narrow on the left, stretch out into broad intervales on the right.

CLINTON.

Though not extensive in territory, Clinton ranks high in the extent, variety, and character of her manufactories. The Lancaster Mills alone cover upwards of four acres of land. The Bigelow Carpet Company, the Clinton Wire-cloth Company, and Harris & Son's Comb Works, have a world-wide reputation. The Worcester & Nashua Railroad crosses the Old Colony in the centre of the village.

LANCASTER,

Situated on the Nashua River, is the oldest town in Worcester County, and one of the most beautiful in the State. It is two miles distant from Clinton, and is reached by carriages, which are constantly in waiting at Clinton station on the arrival of trains. The Nashua River waters a considerable portion of the town, while Fort, Spectacle, White, and Oakhill ponds add to the scenic beauty of the northern section. The principal village is delightfully located near the confluence of the north and south branches of the Nashua. Its streets are shaded with magnificent elms, and smooth, green lawns are seen on every hand. It is a popular vacation resort of many from the metropolis and even more distant places.

STERLING.

At Pratt's Junction, in the northerly village of Sterling, a branch track diverges in a southerly direction, passing through Sterling Centre, a very pretty village, and connecting at Sterling Junction with the Worcester & Nashua Railroad. The Methodist Camp Meeting Grounds are here located on the shores of the beautiful Waushacum Lakes. These grounds are thronged by thousands of people during the annual Camp Meetings. The facilities for boating on the lakes are excellent, while charming views of Wachusett Mountain and Princeton are had from these waters.

LEOMINSTER.

From Pratt's Junction northward, the railroad winds around the base of Pee-kee-wee-kee Hill, a symmetrical, wood-crowned elevation, whose summit is capped with oaks and maples, giving it a peculiar and attractive appearance, and enters the busy and thriving town of Leominster, whose population of five thousand are principally engaged in agricultural and mechanical pursuits. The north branch of the Nashua River, with its affluents, the Monoosnock and Fall brooks, waters the town.

FITCHBURG.

Again striking and continuing along the Nashua River valley a few miles further, the cars reach the new Union Depot in Fitchburg, the most northerly terminus of the Old Colony Railroad. Situated in a beautiful valley, and surrounded by prominent hills, with the Nashua River flowing through its midst, Fitchburg presents a scene of busy activity in its trade and manufactures, which embrace nearly every variety of industry.

Station and Post Office.	Name of House.	Location.	Distance from Station.	Conveyance.	Name of Proprietor.	Time during which kept open.	Price per day.	Price per week.	Capacity.
*Abington	Keene's Hotel	Walnut St.	¼ mile	Carriage	G. R. Keene	Continually	$1.50	$5	50
"	Centennial House	Washington St.	½ "	"	J. H. Jones	"	1.50	5	50
*Acton	Monument House	....	....	....	B. C. Nickerson	Summer	1.25	6 to 10	20
Ashmont Station,	Boarding House	Vanwinkle St.	¼ "	....	B. E. Carlew	....	....	6 to 8	12
Dorchester P.O.	" "	" "	¼ "	....	Mrs. Smith	....	....	6	3
Assonet, Freetown P.O.	Bridge House	Main St.	½ "	Carriage	Mrs. Gardner	Continually	1.00	4.50 to 5	10
*Attleboro	Park St. Hotel	Park St.	Near	Hack	M. A. Davenport	"	2.00	10	100
"	So. Main St. House	So. Main St.	"	"	S. R. Briggs	"	2.00	10	100
*Barnstable	Globe Hotel	Barnstable	"	Carriage	E. H. Eldridge	"	2.00	....	25
*Berlin	Berlin House	Berlin	1 mile	"	John M. Lyons	"	2.00	5 to 7	30
Berlin, Centre P.O.	Cosey Nook	"	½ "	Summer	Willis Rice	Summer	2.00	4 to 6	16
" " "	Boarding House	Berlin Centre	½ "	"	Mrs. N. A. Sawyer	"	2.00	4 to 6	30
" Berlin "	" "	So. Berlin	1 "	"	Mrs. L. R. Hastings	"	2.00	4 to 6	12
*Bolton	Wilder Mansion	Bolton	2½ "	Stage	W. A. Moore	Season	....	....	50
"	Private House	"	2 "	"	E. M. Sawyer	"	....	....	10
"	" "	"	3 "	"	D. J. Nourse	"	....	....	10
"	" "	"	3 "	"	Mrs. M. Z. Taylor	"	....	....	6
"	" "	"	3 "	"	Mrs. Geo. Shrieve	"	....	....	6
" Lancaster P.O.	" "	Lancaster	2 "	Pri. Carriage	E. Avery	"	....	....	15
*Bourne	Boarding House	Good	¼ "	Carriage	J. L. Browne	....	1.00	6	4
"	" "	"	1½ "	"	C. C. Hanley	Summer	1.00	7	4
*Bowenville Station,	Wilbur House	No. Main St.	½ "	{ Horse Cars or Carriage	Geo. K. Wilbur	Continually	2.50	8 to 12	75
Fall River P.O.	Narragansett House	" "	½ "	"	Mrs. R. H. Smith	"	1.50	Varies	50
" "	Dean House	" "	½ "	"	Mrs. N. W. Dean	"	1.50	"	50
" "	Evans House	" "	½ "	"	W. C. Evans	"	1.25	"	30
*Braintree	Boarding House	South of Station	½ "	Carriage.	Geo. Wales	"	....	....	sm'l
"	" "	At Station	⅛ "	"	Mrs. H. Hayward	"	....	....	"
"	" "	"	½ "	"	Mrs. P. Morrison	"	....	....	"
*Brewster	Ocean House	Brewster	1½ "	Barge	Benj. Crocker, 2nd	"	1.00 to 2.00	6 to 10	20
"	Dugan House	"	1 "	"	Mrs. H. C. Dugan	Summer	1.00 to 2.00	6 to 10	35
"	Mansion House	"	1 "	"	H. E. Baker	"	1.00 to 2.00	6 to 10	15
"	Atwood House	"	1 "	"	Atwood Bros.	Continually	1.00 to 2.00	6 to 10	30
"	Brier House	"	1½ "	"	A. F. Brier	"	1.00 to 2.00	6 to 10	25
*Bridgewater	Hyland House	Central Square	½ "	Carriage	L. D. Monroe	"	1.00	6	40
"	Adams House	Near	....	....	Mr. Wade	"	.75	5	20
*Bristol Ferry, R. I.	Bristol Ferry House	"	....	....	Alfred Sisson	"	2.00	10	60

*Western Union Telegraph Office.

PRINCIPAL HOTELS AND BOARDING-HOUSES ON LINE OF OLD COLONY RAILROAD.—*Continued*

Station and Post Office.	Name of House.	Location.	Distance from Station	Conveyance	Name of Proprietor.	Time during which kept open	Price per day.	Price per week	
*Brockton, Mass.	Hotel Belmont	Main St.	1/4	Horse Cars or Carriage	S. P. Howard	Continually	2.00 to 2.50	9 to 12	100
"	Metropolitan Hotel	"	1/8	"	D. D. Clemence	"	2.00	8 to 10	100
"	Holbrook House	"	1/4	"	E. A. Holbrook	"	1.50	6	40
*Buzzard's Bay	Manomet House	Near			Wesley D. Pierce				28
"	Parker House	"	Near		E. O. Parker				24
*Campello	Campello House	Montello St.	Near		G. L. Davenport		1.25	5	45
"	Garfield House	"	"		M. H. Howard		1.00	4	30
"	Montello House	"	"		S. Allen		1.00	4.50	32
"	Tremont House	"	"		G. Kingsley		1.00	4	30
Cataumet	The Jachin	Near Station			A. P. Davis		2.00	7 to 12	60
"	Bay View House		3/4 mile		Fred'k Dimmock		2.00	7 to 12	20
*Chelmsford	Central Hotel	Near Centre	1	Carriage	W. S. Simons	Summer			
"	Summit House	Robbin's Hill	1/2	"	W. S. Simons	Continually			
"	Boarding House	Near Centre	1/4	"	D. N. Russell				
"	Elm House	"	1/2		T. Adams				
*Clinton	Clinton House	Clinton	1/2	Hack	W. W. Cameron		2.00	6 to 12	100
"	Oxford House	"	1/2	"	E. A. Woodward		2.00	6 to 12	60
*Cottage City	Sea View House ·	Oak Bluff's Landing	Near			Summer, European	& American plan.		250
"	Pawnee House	Circuit Ave.	"		Ball & Bassett	Summer	European & Amer. plan		200
"	Island House	"	"		H. H. Hayden	Continually	2.50	15	125
"	Cottage City House	"	"		Mrs. S. A. Stearns	Summer	European & Amer. plan		50
"	Oakwood Cottage	Montgomery Square	"		D. W. Russell	"	"	"	50
"	Central House	Commonwealth Square	"		J. B. Howard		European plan		75
"	Howard House	"	"		A. G. Wesley		2.00 to 2.50		40
"	Wesley House	Siloam Ave.	"		Joseph Dias	Continually	European & Amer. plan		50
"	VineyardGroveHouse	Cottage City	1 mile	Carriage	Charles L. Scranton	Summer	"		50
"	Norton House	Narragansett Ave.	Near				2.00	10	40
"	Hotel Naumkeag	Lagoon Heights	1 mile				European & Amer. plan		200
"	Prospect House	Katama	9		W. D. Carpenter		2.00 to 3.00		150
"	Mattakeeset Lodge	Oak Bluffs		Nar.GaugeRy	Mrs. A. A. Hill				150
Vineyard Highland Landing	The Narragansett	Vineyard Highlands	Near	Carriage	J. C. Alden	Summer	2.00 to 2.50	12 to 15	150
Cottage City P. O.	Highland House	"			Mrs. J. H. Tilton				75
Cottage City	Wyoming House								
Edgartown P. O.	Seaside House	Edgartown	6 miles	Nar.GaugeRy	Geo. A. Smith	Continually	2.00		
"	Boarding House	"	6	"	Mrs. J. D. Coffin	"			
"	"	"	6	"	Mrs. C. M. Teller				

Cottage City, Edgartown P. O.	Boarding House	Edgartown	6 miles	Nar.GaugeRy	A. Osborne	Continually	....	....	....
" "	" "	"	6 "	"	Thos. M. Peakes	"	....	....	....
Cottage City, Edgartown, P. O.	" "	"	6 "	"	Mrs. J. C. Osborne	Summer	....	....	....
Cottage City, Vineyard Haven P.O.	Beach Side	Vineyard Haven	2 "	....	Mrs. Jas. Chase	"	....	....	....
" " "	Boarding House	" "	2 "	....	Mrs. Mary Crocker	"	....	....	....
" " "	Mansion House	" "	2 "	....	Samuel Look	Continually	2.00	....	....
" " "	Grove Hill House	" "	2 "	....	Mrs. L. C. West	"	2.00	....	....
*Cohasset	Pratt's Hotel	Cor. No. & So. Main St.	Near	....	R. C. Davis	"	2.50	12 to 18	75
"	Bates House	Jerusalem Road	1¼ mile	Barge	Warren Bates	"	....	12 to 16	30
"	Beals House	" "	1 "	"	Robert Y. Beal	"	....	10 to 12	25
*Dighton	Boarding House	Dighton	¼ "	Carriage	Mrs. J. A. Negus	"	1.00	5	4
"	" "	"	¾ "	"	Wm. P. Eddy	Summer	1.00	6	6
"	" "	"	¼ "	"	A. R. Barney	"	1.00	5	2
"	" "	"	⅛ "	"	J. F. Lane	Continually	1.00	5	2
*Duxbury	Hollis House	Duxbury	1 "	Coach	J. B. Hollis, Jr.	Summer	2.00	7 to 10	30
"	Brunswick House	"	1 "	"	R. C. Davis	"	2.00	7 to 10	30
*East Marshfield	Boarding House	East Marshfield	¼ "	Barge	J. H. Eames	"	....	75 for seas'n	12
East Milton	" "	East Milton	¼ "	....	H. J. Brokenshire	"	1.00	5	15
" "	" "	"	¼ "	....	J. G. Baxter	"	....	....	8
*East Taunton	Old Colony House	Middleboro' Ave.	⅛ "	....	P. Herbert	....	....	....	....
East Stoughton	Briggs House	East Stoughton	¾ "	Carriage	Mrs. V. Briggs	Summer	1.50	7	40
East Wareham	Onset Bay House	Great Neck	3 "	"	J. H. Burgess	"	1.50	6	40
*East Weymouth	Allan House	East Weymouth	¼ "	"	W. H. Rand	Continually	1.00 to 1.50	7	25
*Fairhaven	Union Hotel	Main St.	⅛ "	....	Wm. Bryden	"	1.00	6	35
*Falmouth	Tower's Hotel	Falmouth Heights	1½ "	Carriage	Geo. Tower	Summer	2.00 to 3.00	10 to 15	150
"	Hotel Falmouth	Falmouth	½ "	"	Geo. W. Fish	Continually	1.50 to 2.00	8 to 12	75
"	Boarding House	Falmouth Heights	1½ "	"	Chas. H. Goodwin	Summer	1.50 to 2.00	8 to 12	35
"	" "	" "	1½ "	"	Sarah J. Brown	"	1.50 to 2.00	8 to 12	20
*Falmouth Sta., Waquoit P.O.	Tobey House	Waquoit	6 "	"	A. P. Tobey	Continually	1.50 to 2.00	8 to 12	15
" " Quissett P.O.	QuissettHarbor House	Quissett Harbor	2 "	"	G. W. Fish	Summer	2.00 to 3.00	10 to 15	125
" " E.Fal'm'h P.O.	Menauhant Hotel	Menauhant	7 "	"	P. A. Roberts	"	2.00 to 3.00	10 to 15	125
Falmouth	Pickwick House	Falmouth Heights	....	"	C. L. Hopson & Co.	"	1.50	7 to 10	....
*Fitchburg	American House	Main St.	Near	"	Geo. H. Cole & Son	Continually	2.00 to 2.50	7 to 10	250
"	Fitchburg Hotel	"	½ mile	"	Judkins & Stetson	"	2.00 to 2.50	7 to 14	200
"	National House	"	½ "	"	J. E. Jacques	"	1.00 to 1.50	4.50 to 12	125
*Fitchburg Sta., Princet'n P.O.	Wachusett House	Princeton	....	"	P. A. Braman & Son	....	2.00	10 to 15	200
" " " "	Summit House	"		TallyHo co'ch	G. H. Derby	Summer	2.50	10 to 15	100
*Foxboro	Cocasset House	Foxboro'	Near	....	M. H. Johnson	Continually	1.00 to 1.50	6	75
*Framingham	Central House	Centre	¼ mile	Carriage	W. C. Wright	"	2.00	7	35
Greenbush	Coleman H'gt's C'tt'ge	Sightly	¼ "	"	A. M. Clement	Summer	....	8 to 15	50
"	Boarding House	Good	½ "	"	Mrs. H. D. Northey	"	....	6 to 12	12

*Western Union Telegraph Office.

Principal Hotels and Boarding-Houses on Line of Old Colony Railroad.—*Continued.*

Station and Post Office.		Name of House.	Location.	Distance from Station.	Conveyance.	Name of Proprietor.	Time during which kept open.	Price per day.	Price per week.	Capacity.
Halifax	Bryantville P. O.	Boarding House	Halifax	2½ mile	....	E. P. Thayer	....	....	....	10
"	" "	" "	Pembroke	1½ "	....	D. Chaudler	....	....	....	6
Halifax		" "	Halifax	3 "	Carriage	S. A. Hewitt	....	....	....	8
*Harwich		Pine Grove Cottage	Harwich	¾ "	Stage	Mrs. D. S. Steele	Continually	1.00 to 2.00	5 to 10	50
"	Harwichport P.O.	Sea View House	Harwichport	1½ "	"	R. Eldridge	Summer	2.00 to 3.00	10 to 15	50
"	Chatham P.O.	Eldridge House	Chatham	8 "	"	A. Eldridge	Continually	1.00 to 1.50	5 to 10	25
"	" P.O.	Traveller's Home	"	8 "	"	S. K. Small	"	1.00 to 1.50	5 to 10	25
"	" P.O.	Lewis House	"	8 "	"	Mrs. Addie Lewis	Summer	1.00 to 2.00	5 to 12	20
"	No. Chatham P.O.	Baxter House	North Chatham	8½ "	"	Mrs. H. L. Baxter	"	1.00 to 2.00	5 to 12	20
"	Chatham P.O.	Howe Cottage	Chatham	8½ "	"	G. H. Howe	"	1.00 to 2.00	5 to 12	25
*Hingham		Rose Standish House	Downer's Landing	2 "	Carriage	Jas. D. Scudder	"	3.00	15 to 30	250
"		Cushing House	Hingham	Near	....	Geo. Cushing	Continually	2.00	10	75
"		Lincoln House	Lincoln St.	½ mile	Carriage	Geo. Harwood	Summer	3.00	10 to 20	50
*Holbrook		Franklin House	Holbrook	1 "	"	H. E. Sawyer	Continually	1.50	7	20
"		Demari House	"	1 "	"	H. H. Demari	"	1.00	7	12
*Hyannis		Iyanough House	Hyannis	⅛ "	"	Mrs. E. H. Davis	"	2.00	7 to 10	50
"		Boarding House	"	¼ "	"	Mrs. A. Bacon	"	1.50	7	25
"		" "	"	¼ "	"	Capt. W. W. Wyer	"	1.50	7	25
Hyannis,	Hyannisport P. O. }	Hallett House	Hyannisport	1½ "	Stage	G. Hallett	Summer	2.00	7 to 10	150
"	" "	Boarding House	"	1½ "	"	Mrs. E. F. Prince	"	....	7 to 10	25
"	" "	" "	"	1½ "	"	Mrs. M. A. Flagg	"	2.00	7 to 10	50
"	" "	" "	"	1½ "	"	J. A. Barnard	"	....	7 to 10	20
"	" "	" "	"	1½ "	"	Mrs. B. K. Wood	"	....	7 to 10	20
"	" "	Pavilion House	"	1½ "	"	Mrs. E. Wheldon	"	....	7 to 10	75
"	Craigville "	Chequaquet House	Craigville	2 "	"	F. B. Washburne	"	....	7 to 10	100
"	" "	Sabin's House	"	2 "	"	Mason Fisher	"	....	7 to 10	75
*Kingston		Patuxet House	Kingston	¼ "	"	A. B. Lucas	Continually	Varies	....	....
Lakeville		Lakeside House	Lakeville	2 "	Private	M. B. Parkhurst	"	1.25	7 to 8	25
"		Lake View House	"	2½ "	"	Sidney T. Nelson	"	1.25	7 to 8	12
"		Woodlawn House	"	4 "	"	C. H. Jewett	"	1.50 to 2.00	8 to 10	30
"		Assawamsett House	"	2 "	"	N. M. Sampson	Summer	1.25	7 to 10	50
*Leominster		Leominster House	Leominster	Near	....	Geo. H. Cole	....	2.00	5 to 10	75
*Lowell		Merrimack House	Merrimack St.	½ mile	Hack	A. V. Partridge	Continually	2.00 to 2.50	6 to 15	175
"		American House	Central St.	½ "	"	Frank E. Shaw	"	2.00 to 2.50	6 to 15	175
"		Washington House	"	½ "	"	Chas. H. Duprez	"	2.00 to 2.50	6 to 15	125
"		St. Charles Hotel	Middlesex St.	½ "	"	Geo. L. Huntoon	"	2.00 to 2.50	6 to 15	152
*Mansfield		Mansfield House	Mansfield	Near	....	C. M. Tibbetts	....	1.50	7	30
"		Day's Boarding House	Rumford Ave.	⅛ mile	....	Alfred B. Day	....	1.50	7	30

*Marlboro'		Windsor House	Main St.	Near	Carriage	L. Houde	Continually	2.00	6 to 10	100
"		Central House	"	"	"	C. F. Barden	"	2.00	7 to 10	100
"		Temple House	"	"	"	Leighton & Hatch	"	1.00 to 2.00	5 to 10	100
"		Maj. Rice House	"	"	"	M. E. West	"	1.25	5 to 6	....
"		Marlboro House	Lincoln St.	½ mile	"	W. H. Leighton	"	1.50	7 to 10	50
"		William's Tavern	Main St.	1 "	"	J. Draper	"	1.50	7 to 10	50
"		Gleason House	"	Near	"	J. M. Gleason	"	1.50	7	50
*Marshfield		Boarding House	Marshfield	⅓ mile	"	H. C. Dunham	"	1.00	5 to 6	15
"		Brown's House	"	1 "	"	D. Brown, Jr.	"	1.00	6	15
"	Brant Rock P.O.	Fair View	Brant Rock	4 "	Barge	M. Swift	Summer	2.00	8 to 12	100
"	" "	Churchill's Hotel	"	4 "	"	Geo. Churchill	"	2.00	8 to 12	250
"	" "	Brant Rock House	"	4 "	"	C. T. Sumner	"	2.00	8 to 12	200
"	" "	Baker's Cottage	"	4 "	"	Mrs. Baker	"	1.00	5 to 6	30
"	" "	Capen House	Ocean Bluff	3½ "	"	S. G. Capen	"	1.00	5 to 6	30
*Marion		Hotel Sippican	Marion	1⅛ "	Stage	C. W. Ripley	"	....	....	....
"		Boarding House	"	1⅛ "	"	Mrs. James Luce	"	....	....	40
"		" "	"	1⅛ "	"	Mrs. C. H. Damon	"	....	....	50
"		" "	"	1⅛ "	"	Obed Delano	"	....	....	25
*Mattapoisett		Mattapoisett House	Mattapoisett	¼ "	Barge	Thos. Madden	Continually	2.00	10 to 14	70
"		Boarding House	"	1-16 "	"	Chas. Barstow	"	1.50	7 to 10	12
"		Barstow House	"	⅓ "	"	Wilson Barstow	Summer	1.50	7 to 10	20
"		Hotel de Potter	"	⅓ "	"	Mrs. E.M.Blanchard	"	1.50	10	10
"		Brandt Island House	"	4 "	"	Brower & Lumis	"	2.00	10 to 14	50
"		Ocean View House	"	¼ "	"	Lilla E. Macconnell	Continually	1.50	10 to 15	20
*Matfield		Nash's Farm	East Bridgewater	1½ "	Coach	F. A. Nash	....	1.50	5 to 8	...
*Medfield		Medfield Hotel	North St.	⅓ "	....	S. Cahoon	Continually	1.50	4.50 to 10	20
"		Central House	"	⅓ "	....	M. G. Barr	"	1.50	5 to 10	30
*Middleboro'		Nemasket House	Main St.	½ "	Hack	P. E. Penniman	Continually	2.00	7	40
"		Boarding House	Centre St.	¼ "	"	C. M. Wilde	"	1.00	6	25
"		" "	Oak St.	¼ "	"	Mary Bryant	"	1.00	5	12
*Milton		" "	School St.	½ "	Carriage	Mrs. Williams	"	No Transn't	10 to 15	20
"		" "	"	½ "	"	Mrs. E. E. Clapp	"	"	8 to 15	15
*Monument Beach		" "		....	....	A. Parker	Summer	2.00	10	20
*Nantucket		The Nantucket	Brant Point	½ "	Carriage & Harbor Str.	J. S. Doyle	"	3.50	12 to 20	300
"		Springfield House	Chester St.	⅛ "	Carriage	A. S. Mowry	Continually	2.00 to 2.50	10 to 17.50	200
"		Surfside Hotel	Surfside	2½ "	Nant. R. R.	....	Summer	3.00	12 to 20	250
"		Ocean House	Cor. Broad & Centre Sts.	⅛ "	Carriage	J. S. Doyle	"	3.00	10 to 20	200
"		Bay View House	Orange St.	½ "	"	....	Continually	2.50 to 3.00	10 to 17	150
"		Veranda House	No. Water St.	⅜ "	"	Mrs. S.G.Davenport	Summer	3.00	10 to 20	150
"		Sherburne House	Orange St.	½ "	"	....	"	2.00 to 2.25	10 to 12	150
"		Wauwinet House	Head of Harbor	7 mile	Carriage & Harbor Str.	Wm. H. Norcross	Summer	2.50	10 to 15	150
"		Central House	Orange St.	½ "	Carriage	....	"	2.00	10 to 12	30

* Western Union Telegraph Office.

Principal Hotels and Boarding-Houses on Line of Old Colony Railroad.—*Continued.*

Station and Post Office.	Name of House.	Location.	Distance from Station.	Conveyance.	Name of Proprietor.	Time during which kept open.	Price per day	Price per week.	Capa-city.
*Nantucket,	Cedar Beach House	Coatue Landing	1 "	Carriage & Harbor Str.	A. W. N. Small	"			
"	Sea Cliff Inn	North St.	¾ "	Carriage	Mrs. C. W. Pettee	"	2.00		125
"	American House								
"	Boarding House	Pearl St.	⅛ "	"	Mrs. E. M. Waitt	Continually	1.50	9 to 10	30
"	" "	Broad St.	Near	"	W. T. Swain	Summer	2.00	12	60
"	" "	"	"	"	Geo. G. Fish	Continually		10.50 to 14	60
"	" "	Centre St.	⅛ mile	"	Mrs. M. J. Austin	Summer	1.50	9 to 10	80
"	" "	Gay St.	⅛ "	"	Capt. David Bunker	"			30
"	" "	Chester St.	⅛ "	"	Mrs. M. Nickerson	"	3.00	10 to 20	30
"	" "				Avis Enos	"			
"	" "				Sarah G. Temple	"			
"	" "				Jane Folger	"			
"	" "				Caroline Swain	"			
"	" "				Lydia Holloway	"			
"	" "				Judith J. Fish	"			
"	" "				Chas. N. Austin	"			
"	" "				Timothy H. Fisher	"			
Nantucket, Siasconset P. O.	Ocean View House	Siasconset	7½ "	Nant. R. R.	Levi S. Coffin	"	3.00	10 to 20	150
" " "	Atlantic House	"	7½ "	"	Mrs. E. Chadwick	"	3.00	12 to 20	75
*New Bedford	Parker House	Purchase St.	½ "	Horse Cars	H. M. Brownell	Continually	2.50 to 3.50	10 to 15	200
" "	Bancroft House	Union St.	½ "	"	N. E. Huggins	"	2.00	7 to 14	125
" "	Mansion House	"	½ "	"	C. W. Ripley	"	2.00	7 to 10	75
New Bedford Station, Nonquitt P. O.	Nonquitt House	Nonquitt, So. Dartm'th	6 "	Steamer	Geo. Hackett	Summer	2.00 to 3.00	12 to 20	80
*Newport, R. I.	Ocean House	Bellevue Ave.	¾ "	Carriage	J. G. Weaver & Son	"	4.00	Varies	400
" "	Aquidneck House	Pelham St.	½ "	"	L. F. Attleton	"	4.00	"	150
" "	Perry House	Washington Square	Near	"	Henry Bull, Jr.	Continually	3.00	"	100
" "	Kay St. Hotel	Kay St.	½ mile	"	Mrs. J. Bateman	Summer			
" "	Cliff Ave Hotel	Cliff Ave.	1 "	"	L. D. Davis, Agt.	"			60
" "	Brayton's Hotel	Pelham St.	½ "	"	J. B. Brayton	Continually			75
" "	Clifton Hotel	Bellevue Ave.	¾ "	"	R. F. Cummings	"	2.50	Varies	70
" "	Boarding House	Church St.	½ "	"	A. A. Wilbur				
Newport, R. I.	Boarding House	Touro St.	½ mile	Carriage	Benj. Nichols				
" "	" "	Catherine St.	¾ "	"	Wm. Riggs				
" "	" "	"	¾ "	"	Chas. T. Hazard				
" "	" "	"	¾ "	"	Wm. Hodges				
" "	Pinard Hotel	Cor. Redw'd & Bellev. av.	½ "	"	Armand Pinard				

Newport, Jamestown P. O.	Conanicut Park Hotel	Jamestown, R. I.	5 "	Steamboat	L. D. Davis, Agt.	Summer	....	....	100
" " "	Gardner House	" "	2 "	Steam Ferry	Gardn'r & Littlefield	Continually	$2.00	Varies	70
" " "	Bay View House	" "	2 "	" "	Chas. T. Knowles	Summer	....	....	70
*North Abington	Culver House	No. Abington	Near	....	A. J. Kimball	Continually	1.50	7	50
*North Acton	Magog House	No. Acton	....	....	E. B. Forbush	"	....	....	....
*Northboro'	Northboro' Hotel	Northboro'	Near	....	Mrs. D. C. Page	"	2.00	5 to 10	40
*North Cohasset, Nantasket P. O.	Hotel Standish	Nantasket Beach	2½ mile	Coach	E. J. Bradley	Summer	3.50	18 to 25	180
	Rockland House	" "	1¾ "	"	Russell & Sturgis	"	4.00	21 to 25	250
" " "	Hotel Nantasket	" "	1¾ "	"	" "	European Plan		....	500
" " "	Atlantic House	Head of Beach	1½ "	"	L. Damon & Son	Summer	2.50 to 3.50	18 to 25	150
" " "	Black Rock House	Jerusalem Road	2½ "	"	....	"	2.00	8 to 12	80
" " "	Konnohasset House	" "	2½ "	"	....	"	....	....	....
" " "	New Pacific House	Centre Hill	2 "	"	W. B. Hathaway	"	2.00 to 3.00	14 to 20	100
" " "	Boarding House	Near	Near	....	Mrs. Lawrie	Continually	1.00	....	....
*North Eastham	Nausett House	No. Eastham	¼ mile	....	John H. Horton	"	1.00	5	....
"	Higgins House	"	¼ "	....	H. Higgins	"	1.00	5	....
"	Hotel Dill	"	¼ "	....	Geo. H. Dill	"	1.00	5	....
North Hanson	Boarding House	No. Hanson	½ "	....	J. Holmes	Summer	....	....	....
"	" "	"	1½ "	....	J. Cobb	"	....	....	....
*North Harwich Station, West Harwich P. O.	Private House	West Harwich	1½ "	Coach	Mrs. H. D. Eldridge	"	1.00	7	20
" " "	Central House	" "	1½ "	"	O. C. Baker	Continually	1.00	7	50
*North Scituate	Mitchell House	Beach	1½ "	Barge	C. H. Mitchell	Summer	1.50	7 to 10	150
"	Florence House	"	1½ "	"	G. M. Davenport	"	1.50	7 to 10	60
"	Centennial House	"	1½ "	"	J. B. Damon	"	1.50	7 to 10	65
*North Truro	Highland House	Highland C. C.	1½ "	....	John W. Small	....	1.00 to 1.50	7	40
"	Pond Village House	No. Truro	Near	....	Isaac Green	....	1.00	5	15
"	Atwood House	"	"	....	Joshua Atwood	....	1.00	6	15
North Weymouth	Bay Side House	No. Weymouth	1½ mile	Barge	Benj. E. Corlew	Summer	2.00	6 to 10	30
"	Litchfield House	Fort Point	2 "	"	Herbert Litchfield	Continually	....	....	20
"	Hotel	"	2 "	....	Benj. Bowen	....	....	....	....
"	Boarding House	No. Weymouth	¼ "	....	Mrs. Chas. E. Briggs	Continually	....	6 to 15	20
"	" "	"	½ "	....	Mrs. Enos White	"	....	6 to 15	10
*Norton	Mansion House	Norton Centre	1 "	Stage	Thos. N. Russell	"	1.50	6 to 10	50
Norton Furnace Sta. Box 313, Taunton.	Farm House	Norton Furnace	⅛ "	....	E. B. Lincoln	Summer	1.00	6	20
Onset Bay Sta., Onset P. O.	Glen Cove House	East Boulevard	1 "	Steam R. R.	Benj. A. Williams	"	2.50	12	100
" " "	Union Villa	Cor. Union av. & Union st.	1 "	"	F. L. Union	"	2.50	12	75
" " "	Hotel Onset	East Boulevard	1 "	"	—— Clarke	"	2.50	12	100
" " "	Hotel Brockton	Onset Ave.	1 "	"	B. J. Keith	"	2.00	10	100
" " "	Washington House	Longwood Ave.	1 "	"	A. W. Washburn	"	1.50	8	100
*Orleans	Shattuck House	Orleans	⅛ "	Carriage	A. B. Shattuck	Continually	1.25	8	25
"	Chandler House	"	½ "	"	James Chandler	"	1.00	7	20
"	Steele House	"	¼ "	"	W. N. Steele	"	1.00	7	10

* Western Union Telegraph Office.

PRINCIPAL HOTELS AND BOARDING HOUSES ON LINE OF OLD COLONY RAILROAD.—*Continued.*

Station and Post Office.	Name of House.	Location.	Distance from Station.	Conveyance.	Name of Proprietor.	Time during which kept open	Price per day.	Price per week.	Capacity.
*Orleans	Boarding House	Orleans	1/4 mile	Carriage	Benj. Higgins	Continually	1.00	7	4
"	" "	"	1/2 "	"	James Smith	"	1.00	7	10
"	" "	"	1/8 "	"	Joseph Snow	"	1.00	7	6
Orleans, East Orleans P. O.	" "	East Orleans	2 "	"	Jonathan Snow	Summer	1.00	7	10
" " "	" "	East Orleans	2 "	"	Freeman Snow	Summer	1.00	7	12
" " "	" "	"	1½ "	"	Mrs.Freeman Doane	"	1.00	7	12
" " "	" "	"	2½ "	"	Oliver Doane	"	1.00	7	12
" " "	" "	"	2 "	"	Benj. Mayo	"	1.00	7	12
" " "	" "	"	2 "	"	Edward Linnell, Jr.	"	1.00	7	8
" " "	" "	"	1½ "	"	Mrs. Mercy Percival	"	1.00	7	10
" " "	" "	"	2 "	"	Hezekiah Taylor	"	1.00	7	4
" " "	" "	"	1¼ "	"	Joseph Mayo	"	1.00	7	6
" " "	" "	Orleans	1 "	"	Francis M. Smith	"	1.00	7	25
" " "	" "	East Orleans	2½ "	"	Mrs.Dinna Freeman	"	1.00	7	4
" So. Orleans "	" "	So. Orleans	2½ "	"	Alva Rogers	"	1.00	7	8
" " "	" "	"	3 "	"	Webster Rogers	"	1.00	7	6
" " "	" "	"	3 "	"	Nelson Rogers	"	1 00	7	6
*Plymouth	Samoset House	Plymouth	Near	"	D. L. Maynard	Continually	2.50	10 to 15	150
"	Clifford House	Head of Beach	3 mile	"	....	Summer	....	....	....
"	Winslow House	Court St.	1/4 "	"	F. A. Johnson	Continually	1.50	5 to 7	75
"	Central House	"	1/4 "	"	M. E. Dodge	"	1.50 to 2.00	5 to 8	60
"	Plymouth Rock Hotel	Coles Hill	1/2 "	"	C. H. Snell	"	1.50 to 2.00	5 to 9	80
"	Churchill House	Central	1/4 "	"	A. R. Churchill	"	1.00	4.50 to 7	50
" Chiltonville P. O.	Franklin House	Near Beach	2 "	"	....	Summer	1.50	....	50
" So. Plymouth P. O.	Manomet House	South Plymouth	7 "	"	....	"	....	....	60
*Provincetown	Gifford House	High St.	1/3 "	Hack	James Gifford	Summer	2.00	10 to 12	50
"	Pilgrim House	Gifford Ave	1/8 "	"	Samuel S. Smith	Continually	1.50 to 2.00	8 to 10	50
"	Central House	Commercial St.	1/4 "	"	Jas. H. Reed, Mang'r	"	1.50 to 2.00	8 to 10	70
"	Atlantic House	Masonic Place	1/3 "	"	Francis P Smith	"	1.50	7 to 10	50
"	Chapman House	Commercial St.	1/4 "	"	Mrs. Chapman	"	1.00	7	10
*Quincy	Robertson House	Quincy	Near	....	J. W. Robertson	"	2.00	6 to 10	75
"	Quincy House	"	"	....	G. A. Ordway	"	1.50	6 to 9	30
"	Mears House	Hough's Neck	6 mile	Stage	Jas Mears	Summer	2.00	6 to 10	25
" Quincy Point P. O.	Linden House	" "	5 "	"	J. D. Taber	"	2.00	6 to 10	50
" " "	Fairview House	No. Weymouth	2 "	"	Lewis Bond	"	2.00	6 to 10	25
*Randolph	Howard House	Randolph	½ "	Carriage	W. B. Hathaway	Continually	1.50	6	60
"	Winslow House	"	Near	"	Mrs. L. C. Winslow	"	1.00	5 to 6	30
Raynham	Nippenickett House	Near Lake	2 mile	"	W. P. Ayer	"	2.00	7 to 9	28
*Sagamore	Boarding House	View of Cape Cod Bay	1/8 "	"	L. S. Savery	Summer	1.00	7	10

*Sandwich	Central House	Main St.	¼ mile	Carriage	A. C. Southworth	Summer	1.50 to 2.00	9	20
"	Shawnee House	Jarvis St.	⅛ "	"	Harry Hack	"	1.00	7	20
"	Boarding House	Main St.	¼ "	"	Mrs. L. A. Spring	"	1.50 to 2.00	7	10
"	" "	Jarvis St.	⅛ "	"	Mrs. S. Rogers	"	1.00	7	10
"	" "	Grove St.	½ "	"	Arthur Braman	"	1.00 to 1.50	9	10
"	" "	School St.	½ "	"	Mrs. Linehin	"	1.00 to 1.50	9	10
Saviu Hill, Dorchester Dist. P. O.	Tuttle House	Savin Hill	¼ "	....	L. M. Noble	"	....	8	10
*Scituate	So. Shore House	Front St.	1 "	Barge	J. E. Merritt	"	1.00 to 2.00	6 to 12	50
"	Scituate House	First Cliff	2 "	"	John Lyons	"	1.00 to 2.00	6 to 10	25
"	Seaside House	Willow St.	1 "	"	P. Murphy	"	....	6 to 10	15
"	Fourth Cliff House	Fourth Cliff	3 "	"	W. E. Merritt	"	....	6 to 10	15
"	Satuit Spring House	Willow St.	1 "	"	Rufus Clapp	"	....	6 to 9	15
"	Satuit House	Front St.	1 "	"	Mrs E. Bowditch	"	....	6 to 9	13
"	Boarding House	Central St.	½ "	"	Mrs. S. Newell	"	....	6 to 9	8
"	" "	Willow St.	1 "	"	J. W. Tilden	"	....	6 to 9	7
"	" "	Central St.	½ "	"	J. Edson	"	....	6 to 9	6
"	" "	Front St.	1 "	"	Mrs. N. Torrey	"	....	6 to 9	6
"	" "	"	1 "	"	Mrs. J. Poole	"	....	6 to 9	6
"	" "	First Cliff	2 "	"	Mrs. Conroy	"	....	6 to 9	7
"	" "	Central St.	1-6 "	"	Walter Merritt	Continually	....	5 to 8	2
*Sea View	Hotel Humarock	Humarock Beach	1½ "	"	....	....	....	....	250
"	Riverside Cottage	Near Humarock Beach	1¼ "	"	Mrs. C. F. Ames	Summer	1.50	8 to 10	10
"	Freedom House	Humarock Beach	1¼ "	"	....	"	1.50	8 to 10	30
"	Sea View House	....	Near	"	G. A. Taylor	"	1.50	8 to 10	30
*Southboro'	Elm House	Southboro'	"	....	J. W. Hammond	Continually	2.00	Transient 14	....
*South Braintree	Boarding House	Cor. Pearl & Hancock Sts	½ mile	....	A. Z. Howe	"	1.25	5	15
" "	" "	Crescent Ave.	¼ "	....	R. Sanborn	"	1.25	5	10
" "	" "	Central St.	½ "	....	Mrs. Clara Penniman	"	1.25	5	7
" "	" "	Cor. Depot & Hanc'ck sts	¼ "	....	Mrs. C. E. Smart	"	European Plan		....
" "	" "	Depot St.	⅛ "	....	Mrs. F. L. Adams	"	1.00	5	8
*South Dennis	Nickerson House	South Dennis	Near	....	Mrs. L. B. Nickerson	"	1.00	5	24
" East Dennis P. O.	Sears House	East Dennis	4½ mile	Carriage	Mrs. Ella Sears	"	1.00	5	10
East Dennis P. O.	Chapman House	"	4 "	"	Samuel Chapman	"	1.00	5	5
*South Duxbury Standish Shore P. O.	Standish House	South Duxbury	1¼ mile	Barge	F. H. Palmer	Summer	2.50	8 to 15	125
*South Framingham	Old Colony House	South Framingham	Near	....	Frank Brooks	Continually	2.00	7	50
"	Coburn House	" "	¼ mile	....	W. H. Miller	"	1.50	5	60
"	So. Framingham Hotel	" "	Near	....	W. G. Morse	"	2.00	6	35
"	Everett House	" "	¼ mile	....	C. P. Jackson	"	1.00	4.50	30
"	Haynes House	" "	Near	....	G. H. Eames	"	1.50	5	45
"	Winthrop House	" "	"	....	L. A. Bruce & Co.	"	1.50	6	40
South Hanson	Boarding House	Good	⅛ mile	Coach	S. F. Josselyn	"	....	4	10
" "	" "	"	⅓ "	"	Mrs. C. Thomas	"	....	4	10

* Western Union Telegraph Office.

Principal Hotels and Boarding-Houses on Line of Old Colony Railroad.—*Continued.*

Station and Post Office.	Name of House.	Location.	Distance from Station.	Conveyance.	Name of Proprietor.	Time during which kept open.	Price per day	Price per week.	Capacity.
South Hanson	Boarding House	Good	1 mile	Coach	I. Stetson	Continually	....	4	5
" "	" "	"	1 "	Carriage	C. O. Thomas	"	....	4	5
*South Sudbury	Boarding House	South Sudbury	Near	....	C. A. Cutter	Continually	1.00	5	5
" "	" "	" "	"	....	J. P. Allen	"	1.00	4.50	4
" " Wayland P. O.	Pequod House	Wayland	3 mile	Cent. Mass RR	C. Loker	"	1.00	5	20
" "	Heard House	South Sudbury	½ "	Express	Mrs. George Heard	"	1.00	4.50	7
South Wellfleet	Pond Hill House	South Wellfleet	⅛ "	Carriage	Geo. P. Rogers	"	1.00	5.00	18
" "	Cambridge House	" "	⅛ "	"	Joseph Pierce	Summer	1.00	5.00	25
*South Weymouth	Cushing House	Main St.	¾ "	Barge	Wm. M. Cushing	Continually	1.00	6.00	15
" "	Weymouth Hotel	Pond St.	⅛ "	"	T. R. Newell	"	1.00	6.00	25
*South Yarmouth	Hawes House	South Yarmouth	2 "	Stage	Mrs. L. Hawes	....	1.00	6.00	....
" "	Boarding House	" "	2 "	"	Allen B. Baker	....	....	....	....
" "	" "	" "	2 "	"	Mrs. C. Baxter	....	....	....	....
" "	" "	" "	2 "	"	Fred. A. Baker	....	....	....	....
" "	" "	" "	2 "	"	Mrs. Addie Cole	....	....	....	....
" "	" "	Lower Village	3 "	"	I. F. Homer	....	....	....	....
" "	" "	" "	3 "	"	Hebron Matthews	....	....	....	....
" "	" "	" "	3 "	"	Isaiah Sherman	....	....	....	....
" "	" "	"	3 "	"	Mrs. W. H. Brown	....	....	....	....
*Stoughton	Stoughton House	Stoughton Centre	1 "	"	William Keith	Continually	1.25	7	30
"	Boarding House	" "	½ "	"	E. W. Dean	Summer	1.25	7	60
"	" "	" "	1 "	"	Mrs. John Guild	Continually	1.25	7	30
"	" "	" "	1 "	"	S. A. W. Parker	"	1.25	7	30
*Sterling	Central House	Sterling	⅛ "	....	J. N. Brooks	"	1.50	6	18
*Sudbury	Highland House	Sudbury	⅛ "	....	J. S. Hunt	"	1.50	10	6
"	Boarding House	"	¼ "	....	Mrs. G. Parmenter	"	1.50	8	10
Swansea	Thurston House	Gardner's Neck	¼ "	Carriage	E. M. Thurston	Summer	....	....	15
*Taunton	Westminster Hotel	Cohanett St	¼ "	Horse cars	R. W. Hunton	Continually	2.00	12	60
"	Hotel Bristol	"	⅛ "	"	Francis Brothers	"	1.50	8	40
"	City Hotel	City Square	¼ "	"	Floyd Travis	"	2.50	7 to 20	150
*Tiverton, R. I.	Boarding House	Shore	½ "	Carriage	Mrs. A. Snell	"	1.00 to 1.50	7 to 10	10
*Tremont, Mass, West Wareham P. O.	" "	Rochester	¾ "	Private	Mrs. C. C. Gurney	"	....	5	10
	" "	West Wareham	¾ "	"	Mrs. A. Morse	"	1.25	5	10
*Truro	Bay View House	Truro	¼ "	....	Benj. H. Paine	Summer	1.00	5	12
"	Cardis House	"	1½ "	....	Chas. Cardis	"	1.00	5	12
"	Ryder House	"	1¼ "	....	Mrs. Solomon Ryder	"	1.00	5	6
*Walpole	Walpole House	Central	Near	Carriage	W. J. Horner	Continually	2.00	7 to 10	50
*Warren, R. I.	Coles Hotel	Cor. Main & Joyce Sts.	"	"	Jeremiah Goff	"	2.00	6 to 9	50
" "	Fessenden House	Cor. Main & Croade Sts.	"	"	Geo. L. Crump	"	1.50 to 2.00	6 to 9	40

Town / P.O.	House	Location	Dist.	Conveyance	Proprietor	Season	Rate	Hours	No.
*Wareham, Mass.	Thompson House	Wareham	"	Carriage	Mrs. E. A. Howes	Continually	2.00	7 to 10	30
"	Wankinko House		"	"	Jas. Galligar	"	2.00	7 to 10	35
"	Kendrick House		"	"	Albert Shaw	"	2.00	10 to 12	30
*Webster Place, " Green Harbor P. O.	Mabel Cottage	Green Harbor	2 mile	"	Willard Houghton	Summer	2.00	10 to 12	30
"	Webster House	"	2 "	"	Lot. J. Madan	Continually	2.00	10 to 12	50
"	Boarding House	"	2 "	"	Geo. J. Peterson	Summer	1.50	8 to 12	70
"	Winslow House	"	2 "	"	Isaac W. Cole	Summer	1.50	8 to 12	70
*Wellfleet	Holbrook House	Centre	¼	"	L. M. Godfrey	Continually	1.50	8 to 10	10
"	Boarding House	"	⅓	"	Mrs. Lot Hall	"	1.00	6	....
"	Boarding House		Near	"	Zoeth Nickerson	"	1.00	6	....
*West Barnstable	Crosby House	Osterville	6 mile	Stage	H. S. Crosby	Summer	1.50	8 to 10	40
" Osterville P. O.	Bay View House	Cotuit	6	"	Mrs. J. R. Nickerson	Continually	1.25	7 to 10	20
" Cotuit	Crosby House	Centreville	5	"	A. S. Crosby	"	1.25	8 to 10	25
" Centerville	Santuit House	Cotuit	6	"	Jas. Webb	Summer	2.00	8 to 14	60
" Cotuit	Boarding House		6	"	Andrew Lovell	"	2.00	10 to 12	20
" Osterville	Cotocheset House	Osterville	6	"	Mrs. Granville Ames	"	2.00	10 to 14	175
*West Falmouth	Boarding House	Main St.	½		J. D. Hoxie		1.00		6
*Weymouth	Boarding House	Weymouth	½	Carriage	C. F. Vaughn				....
"		"	¼	"	Mrs. L. H. Loud				....
"		"	¼	"	Mrs. E. White				....
*Whitman	Hobart House	South Ave.	½	"	S. M. Watts	Continually	1.50	8	75
"	Bates House	Washington St.	¾	"	M. R. Shaw	"	1.50	7	60
"	Pratt House		¾	"	H. H. Pratt	"	1.50	7	20
*Wollaston	Wollaston Hotel	Wollaston	Near		S. A. Merrill		2.00		70
*Woods Holl	Dexter House	Woods Holl			H. M. Dexter		2.00	10	20
*Yarmouth Station, Yarmouthport P. O.	Boarding House	Centre of Village	½ mile	Stage	Mrs. Susan Crocker				5
"	"	"	½	"	Mrs. S. A. Hallett		1.25		5
"	"	"	½	"	Mrs. E. Ryder		1.25		5
" Dennis	Tobey Farm	Dennis	5	"	Mrs. E. H. Lewis	"	1.00	6 to 7	15
"	Boarding House	"	5	"	Nathan Hall	Summer	1.00		8
"	"	"	5	"	Joseph Sylvan	"	1.00		10
"	"	"	5	"	Ansel Howes	"	1.00		14
"	"	"	5	"	Mrs. Amanda Hall	"	1.00		4
"	"	"	5	"	Cyrus Hall	"	1.00		5
"	"	"	5	"	Jeremiah Howes	"	1.00		5
"	Nobscusett House	"	5½	"	C. W. Ripley		1.50	8 to 18	150

⇢ HOW TO GET THERE. ⇠

From New York, the Steamers of the Fall River Line leave Pier 28 North River, foot of Murray Street, every afternoon, (Sundays included, except from January to April), for Newpoi Fall River, connecting at latter point with trains of the Old C Railroad for Boston, Lowell, Fitchburg, Cape Cod, New Bedfor all points on the Old Colony system. Passengers for Martha's Vir and Nantucket connect at New Bedford with Steamer, landing th the Islands same morning.

From Boston, trains leave week-days (and Sundays in Summer) Old Colony R.R. Station.

From Fitchburg, Lowell, South Framingham, Mansfield, Wi etc., daily, Sundays excepted.

For time-tables, passengers are referred for the latest inforr to the official time-tables and folders of the Fall River and Old C Lines, and to the *Pathfinder Railway Guide*. The latter can be l any newsdealer for twenty-five cents, or by addressing *Path* Boston. The *Official Guide*, published in New York, and the McNally *Guide*, published in Chicago, also contain latest time-i

Copies of this book, time-tables, and any particular inforn desired in regard to the Line, will be cheerfully and prompti nished on application.

J. H. FRENCH, *Supt. Main Line Div. O. C. R.R., Boston, Mai*
I. N. MARSHALL, *Supt. North Div. O. C. R.R., Fitchburg*
C. H. NYE, *Supt. Cape Cod Div. O. C. R.R., Hyanni*
L. H. PALMER, *Agent Fall River Line, Boston,*
G. W. MILLER, *Agent O. C. R.R., Lowell,*
B. F. KINGSBURY, *Agent O. C. R.R., Taunton, Mass.*
W. B. FISHER, *Agent O. C. R.R., New Bedford, Mass.*
A. L. ACKLEY, *Agent Fall River Line, Fall River*
J. H. JORDAN, *Agent Fall River Line, Newi*

GEORGE L. CONNOR, General Passenger Agent, New York and

J. R. KENDRICK, General Manager, Boston.

www.ingramcontent.com/pod-product-compliance
Lightning Source LLC
Chambersburg PA
CBHW032153010726
47493CB00008BA/2686